The African Prince, the Translator, and the Nazi

a novel

Didier Leclair

Translated by Phyllis Aronoff and Howard Scott

MAWENZI
HOUSE

We acknowledge the support of the Canada Council for the Arts for our publishing program. We also acknowledge support from the Government of Ontario through the Ontario Arts Council, and the support of the Government of Canada through the Canada Book Fund.

Originally published in French as Le prince africain, le traducteur et le nazi by Les Éditions David, Ottawa, Canada.

Cover Design: Peggy Stockdale
Cover image: Max 5799/iStock.com

Library and Archives Canada Cataloguing in Publication

Title: The African prince, the translator and the Nazi : a novel / Didier Leclair ; translated by Phyllis Aronoff and Howard Scott.

Other titles: Prince africain, le traducteur et le nazi. English

Names: Leclair, Didier, author. | Aronoff, Phyllis, 1945- translator. | Scott, Howard, 1952- translator.

Description: Translation of: Le prince africain, le traducteur et le nazi. | In English, translated from the French.

Identifiers: Canadiana (print) 20260256277 | Canadiana (ebook) 20260256781 | ISBN 9781774152225 (softcover) | ISBN 9781774152249 (PDF) | ISBN 9781774152232 (EPUB)

Subjects: LCGFT: Historical fiction. | LCGFT: Thrillers (Fiction) | LCGFT: Novels.

Classification: LCC PS8573.E3385 P7513 2026 | DDC C843/.6,Äîdc23

Printed and Bound in Canada by Coach House Printing

Mawenzi House Publishers
192 Spadina Avenue
Toronto, ON M5T 2C2
Canada
www.mawenzihouse.com

For Chester Himes, the unforgettable

For Serge Cimpaye, my lifelong brother

Contents

A Prince at the Gare du Nord

The Gare du Nord was teeming with Parisians and foreigners, walking quickly, their eyes filled with fear. It was November 1941 and Paris, under the Occupation, was full of people wanting to get out. Some had proper visas, others had only forged documents that wouldn't pass inspection by the German soldiers. who were patrolling the station with their dogs. The people on the wide platforms could scarcely conceal their trepidation.

Jean de Dieu, translator for an Angolan prince, was accompanying his employer to the first-class car of a train to Lisbon. The employer was His Highness Antonio Jose Henrique Dos Santos Mbwafu of the Kingdom of Kongo. He was one of the sons of the Kongolese monarch, who had been on the throne since 1923.

The Kingdom of Kongo was located in the territory of Angola. It had shrunk in size as a result of the slave trade and Portuguese colonization. It was governed by a certain Pedro VII. To tell the truth, he did not govern much. The Portuguese government paid him a stipend and he was responsible for resolving local conflicts among his subjects, such as disputes about livestock. Portugal tolerated his presence in order to ease tensions with the native population, which maintained a semblance of dignity by having a symbolic sovereign.

The prince's father had had eight wives and some twenty children. Before ascending to the throne, he'd had to convert to Catholicism and marry just one of his wives in accordance with the Catholic rite of marriage. He had kept the other wives in the background. When it came time to think about an eventual successor, he had chosen the eldest of all his children and sent him to be educated in Europe.

Prince Antonio said to Jean de Dieu in Swahili, "You'll find the rent money in the back of my bedroom closet, and make sure you pay the coal merchant. Above all, avoid hanging around outside at night, you never know."

The young man answered with deference and helped his employer, who was only twenty-five years of age, climb into his compartment, holding his ivory-headed cane. The middle-class passersby kept glancing at them, curious about this elegant African who was wearing flannel pants with wide cuffs and Richelieu shoes polished to perfection. His striped blue blazer with gold buttons was made to measure, and his forest green tweed coat had wide lapels displaying the coat of arms of the Kingdom of Kongo and the Portuguese bicolour flag with its armillary sphere. Black leather gloves were sticking out of his upper pocket. It was difficult to find leather in occupied Paris, but that did not seem to have been a problem for the prince. Before disappearing inside the train, he made a show of doffing his Homburg and allowing a mature lady who was looking for her seat to pass in front of him. Jean de Dieu quickly stepped back onto the platform and waved to the prince one last time.

"Safari njema! Bon voyage!" he cried as the train started to move, hoping His Highness would hear him. Prince Antonio did hear him because he thanked him, barely audibly over the noise of the engine, "Asante!"

His Highness was to return in three or four weeks at the latest. It was a business trip. He was going to the port of Lisbon to pick up a shipment of coffee from Angola that his father, His Excellency Pedro VII, had instructed him to sell to local merchants. The king had obtained permission to do so from the Portuguese authorities, because the meagre stipend from the colonial government could not provide for all the needs of his huge family.

Jean de Dieu had quickly understood, given his employer's lifestyle, that the prince did not depend solely on his father's coffee. He had realized on his very first day in the job that Prince Antonio was engaged in diamond trafficking. He had questioned the prince, who had confirmed it without the least hesitation and explained, with a certain eloquence, that the looting of Africa by the colonists was a great deal more reprehensible than his business. According to him, he was only taking advantage of what his mother country had in her belly.

The prince appreciated his employee's perspicacity and gave him a role as his representative. Jean de Dieu had to question every visitor regarding their identity and the purpose of their visit. If the client spoke French, he would translate out loud into Swahili. Prince Antonio, listening in another room, would press a button for a green light to let the client in. A red light had the opposite meaning, and Jean de Dieu would advise the visitor to leave before things got messy. He could be quite convincing with a gun in his hand.

The visitors, Swiss or Russian diamond dealers, were willing to pay exorbitant prices. Jeweller's loupes to their eyes, they would peer at the stones and take out wads of cash.

Officially, Jean de Dieu had met Antonio's father, the King, in the Belgian Congo three years earlier. His Excellency had gone there to find someone to assist his son by translating his courses at the Institut d'Ethnologie while he was learning French. He wanted to provide Prince Antonio with a solid knowledge of African cultures so that he could one day replace him on the throne.

The prince had been in Europe for five years. He had tried studying economics in Lisbon, but that had been a failure. Paris and ethnology were his second attempt at obtaining a university degree. In actual fact, his university enrollment was only a pretext in order to obtain a visa. Prince Antonio's trafficking operation also involved King Pedro VII, who sent him the stones hidden in bags of coffee.

On the recommendation of a Belgian Catholic missionary who had seen in Jean de Dieu "a native endowed with greater intelligence than his fellow students," he had been sent to Lisbon to join the prince. They had made the journey to Paris together by train.

During three years in Paris, Prince Antonio never attended classes. He spent his time meeting with clients of his smuggling operation and Angolan compatriots seeking various favours. He played the role of an Angolan consul more than anything else. Jean de Dieu had started studying in his place, because he found ethnology fascinating. He would go to the Institut pretending to be Prince Antonio with his employer's approval.

Return to Prince Antonio's Apartment

Although he feared that he was under surveillance, Jean de Dieu strode confidently out of the Gare du Nord. The Reich Security Main Office (RSHA), which was part of the notorious Schutzstaffel (SS), had been taking an interest in Prince Antonio's activities in recent months. The prince was making money that was not being declared, which aroused the envy of the German officers, who saw a juicy opportunity to cash in by blackmailing the Angolan.

The translator was the same age as the prince and, curiously, they shared the same date of birth. The similarities ended there. Unlike his employer, with his prominent facial features and square shoulders, the translator looked like one of those male fashion models, tall and slender, with fine features. Heavy-lidded eyes, often hidden behind sunglasses, an aquiline nose, and lips that were very dark, as were his gums, which were visible when he smiled. His height, over a metre eighty, and his natural vitality often intimidated people. He moved with ease and looked at people with a penetrating, inquisitive gaze.

The translator came from an elite group in the Belgian Congo known as the évolués. Beginning in the thirties, the Belgian colonists needed educated Africans. They paid them peanuts and used them to perform office duties. Jean de Dieu, who had been training for the priesthood, had switched to colonial administration when he was eighteen and found that the temptations of the flesh in Léopoldville, the colonial capital, were much stronger than his religious faith. He was first recruited to correct official documents in the office of the Belgian governor. Then he spent a year as translator for a Flemish cartographer who was travelling with porters in the Congo savannah. He translated Lingala and Swahili as well as Kikongo. He also understood German, which had been taught to him by a Flemish priest at the minor seminary. He told his former German teacher that he was dying of boredom in the bush with the cartographer. Shortly after that, the teacher thought of him when Pedro VII came knocking on his door. That was in 1938.

Jean de Dieu stopped and lit a Gitane in front of a propaganda poster that read, "Abandoned people, put your trust in the German soldier!" and showed three children with a soldier of the Wehrmacht who looked protective and reassuring. He walked past a few taxis, which were fueled by wood or charcoal. Farther on, he avoided two bicycle taxis that had just picked up customers. He signaled to the driver of a beige Renault Celtaquatre with chrome headlights. The car looked almost new, although they were no longer being made because of the war. Gleaming bodywork, sloping grille, streamlined design, bench seat with a removable velvet cover. The spoked wheels came to a stop in front of Jean de Dieu as he was brushing off the ash that had fallen on his off-white wool coat.

Like the car, Jean de Dieu looked classy. He was wearing brown trousers embroidered with chevrons, a double-breasted jacket of the same colour, a white shirt with cufflinks, and a blue tie. His hat was a beige fedora with a black ribbon. All this was the result of Prince Antonio's influence. Before knowing him, Jean de Dieu had dressed soberly in the modest manner that had been instilled in him at the minor seminary. Since then, a lot of water had passed under the bridge.

The driver's name was Hans and he also worked for Prince Antonio. Hans often acted as bodyguard. He searched the diamond customers before their meetings with Prince Antonio and stood behind the prince during financial transactions. At the slightest suspicious movement, he would pull out his weapon. Originally from Mainz, a city in the southern Rhineland, this half-German hated the grey-green uniforms that had proliferated in Paris. For good reason. He belonged to the community that bore the unfortunate label of "Rhineland bastards." With a Senegalese father who had been a soldier, and a mother who was white, Hans had had a difficult childhood because of the colour of his skin.

His father had been among the colonial troops occupying the Rhineland after Germany's defeat in the First World War. Hans hadn't seen him since the age of seventeen. That had been five years ago. As for his mother, she had died from a pulmonary embolism. Her last wish, whispered to her son, was that he find his father, Mamadou, who must be somewhere in France according to the last letters she had received.

Once they were in power, the Nazis had forbidden Germans to fraternize with Afro-Germans, and when Hans received a summons from the Sipo-SD, the German security police, he knew what it was about: Hitler's program of forced sterilization of the thousands of mixed-blood Germans. Hans had taken refuge in Paris.

Jean de Dieu got in beside the driver and said, "To HQ, Hans."

The driver put on a smile and started the car. He knew what that meant. The translator was going to enjoy his employer's beautiful apartment, drinking black-market champagne and smoking cigars. He had the approval of Prince Antonio, who definitely did not want his translator to stray too far from his safe, which was in the back of his closet, behind all the stylish clothes.

Hans was relaxed when Prince Antonio was away. He knew that Jean de Dieu could defend himself. He had given him a Ruby pistol, a French-made semi-automatic, with an ankle holster, and had taught him to shoot in the countryside far from Paris. Hans himself had a Luger, a 9 mm with an ivory grip, tucked in the small of his back.

Hans was avoiding speeding. They took Boulevard Barbès, then Porte de Clignancourt, and the car was humming along nicely. Hans took great care of it, because he knew that if ever he was pursued by one of the SS front-wheel-drive vehicles, it would take a car in good condition to get away.

Thanks to Prince Antonio, Hans had the best false papers you could get in Paris under the Occupation. His Highness had paid a small fortune for them. The forger, a former member of the judicial police, a notorious Communist, had given him the name Jules Montlouis and

French nationality. There was a stamp from the National Police overlapping his photo, as required.

As for Jean de Dieu, he had a Portuguese identity card, "Republica Portuguesa," that Prince Antonio had given him when they were on the train to Paris.

"Your name is now João de Deus Kassoma. You're from the colony of Angola, and you're my translator and private secretary. Your residency visa is in order," His Highness had said without waiting for his response.

Jean de Dieu had politely requested the reason for the false papers. His Highness had explained that he'd had some "administrative difficulties" with the French authorities and in order to spare himself any further such annoyances, it was better to do things this way. That was before Jean de Dieu discovered his employer's actual occupation.

The translator had accepted the situation. He certainly did not want to get on the boat back to the Belgian Congo. He had nearly died of boredom with the cartographer, who named every river and waterway after gods from Greek mythology. He lived in a small apartment on Rue Grégoire-de-Tours. His name was Jean de Dieu N'kuba, from the Belgian colony of Ruanda-Urundi, two tiny territories right beside the big Congo.

Hans parked the Renault in an alley a few minutes from the prince's apartment. Jean de Dieu got out first. Hans stayed in the car and stared in the rear-view mirror. Then he followed at some distance.

Jean de Dieu took the stairs up to the third floor. Hans followed silently behind like a cat. They didn't meet anyone in the corridor. Once inside the apartment, the translator went directly to his employer's bedroom. Two days before, he had promised to give Hans his salary. Hans intended to buy himself a new suit to wear to a jazz show at a club in Pigalle.

Jean de Dieu tossed him a wad of bills he had taken out of the safe. "I've added a little bonus."

"Thank you, I'll drink to your health."

Jean de Dieu closed the safe and went into the living room with his friend. For an apartment under the Occupation, the whole place was furnished opulently. Louis XIV furniture with worn gilding and azure blue cushions, a Persian carpet, a walnut dining table, a piano in the corner that was gathering dust, and especially, a bar in the shape of a sphere. There was a portrait of the King of Kongo on one wall and opposite it, a photograph of Prince Antonio in full dress uniform. The translator took a bottle of brandy and two goblets out of the open sphere. The liquor, purchased illegally, had no label. It burned their throats and stung their eyes, sensations they were seeking that winter morning.

The clock struck ten and the cuckoo emerged for its little show without the two men paying any attention to it. They were used to it.

Hans pulled open the heavy piped drapes and glanced out the window, and the daylight made him squint. "Another beautiful day to stay alive," he said to himself. He left without another word.

Jean de Dieu watched Hans disappear around the corner of the street and decided to take a bath. He heated the water on the coal stove and carefully carried several pitchers of it to the bathtub, which was big enough to accommodate his long legs. He added a little cold water and got in, holding a book and a cigar. The steaming water relaxed him, and the cigar created wreaths of grey smoke above his head. He had turned on the Pathé suitcase gramophone and lowered the needle onto a record by Charles Trenet, which he had purchased so that his employer could practise his French. But Prince Antonio played it only to impress the shopgirls who visited him.

> *Boum ! Quand notre coeur fait boum, tout avec lui dit boum ! Et c'est l'amour qui s'éveille ! [Boom! When your heart goes boom, everything with it says boom! And it's love that awakens!]*

He was listening absentmindedly, since his schoolbook German required him to read slowly and the book in his hands demanded his concentration. It was entitled *Theory of Human Heredity and Racial*

Hygiene. Written by the Nazi ethnologist Fritz Lenz and published in the thirties, it was on Prince Antonio's program of study. Jean de Dieu was making an effort to understand his enemies' flawed methods of analysis. He had no illusions; the war was here to stay. The Führer had broken the Munich Agreement of 1938. And Jean de Dieu had never believed that he would respect the non-aggression pact with the Soviets. It was now four months since Hitler had sent his army to invade the USSR: Operation Barbarossa. "That man will never stop. He will have to be liquidated," concluded Jean de Dieu, drawing on his cigar. He continued diligently reading his book. Understanding the Nazi intellectuals gave him an advantage. He knew their obsessions, whereas they knew nothing about him. For the Nazi ethnologists, Africa was a treasure trove where you could just help yourself, and Africans were animals with a gift for mimicry. Jean de Dieu was fascinated by the extent of their ignorance.

Charles Trenet suddenly stopped singing, and Jean de Dieu heard footsteps in the living room. He tossed his book down onto the tile floor of the bathroom and put his cigar out in the water, then stood up to climb out of the tub. His hand moved towards the drawer under the mirror across from him. His employer kept a loaded revolver there. But he didn't have time to get a hold of it. A German soldier was pointing an automatic pistol at him. Completely naked, Jean de Dieu put his hands up. The soldier motioned to him to get out of the tub and ordered him in German to hurry up. His heart was pounding and his eyes were fixed on the end of the gun barrel as if that could keep the man from firing at him.

The soldier grabbed the book with its wet pages and pushed Jean de Dieu into the living room, still with nothing on his body and his hands in the air. Two more soldiers, armed with submachine guns in firing position, were waiting for orders from a major, who had his back turned, observing the lovely view of Paris out the window.

The major turned around and Jean de Dieu saw a middle-aged man, perhaps in his late fifties, clean-shaven, a monocle in his right eye and a pout of disgust on his thin, pale lips. He was rather overweight, but his stiff posture almost hid it. He took his time observing the dripping translator. His face didn't change. Then he put his gloved hands on the African's torso and looked at his index finger as if to check if his colour had rubbed off. The soldier showed him what Jean de Dieu had been reading and the major nodded. He could see who he was dealing with. An intellectual aristocrat. The major exhaled loudly to express his exasperation. "Prince Antonio?"

"Uhh, no."

The officer glanced quickly at his guards and one of them struck Jean de Dieu on the chin with the butt of his gun. The African barely had time to raise his arms to protect himself. He felt his lower lip swelling almost immediately, and grimaced with pain. He was shivering with the cold but the officer paid no attention to that.

"Major F. Baumeister," he said by way of introduction.

He circled the African as if he was some mysterious extraterrestrial. "I'll start again," he said warningly. "Prince Antonio?"

This time, Jean de Dieu simply pointed to the photograph of the prince that was prominently displayed opposite the portrait of his father wearing a crown and holding a sceptre.

The major went over to the photo of the prince. "You're the one who attends the Institut d'Ethnologie, aren't you?"

"Yes, I'm attending classes. But I'm not Prince Antonio."

"Your name?"

"João de Deus Kassoma, Prince Antonio's translator."

The major turned to one of his soldiers and said in German, "So these people take baths in their employer's apartment? It's not possible."

The translator acted as if he hadn't understood a word.

"Papers," ordered Baumeister.

Jean de Dieu motioned that he had to get them from his clothes in the bathroom. The major nodded. Jean de Dieu hurried to the other room and put on his pants under the vigilant gaze of a soldier. He returned with his papers in hand. The major looked at them with the same disdain as before. He could take this African in for interrogation immediately. But he considered him small fry. A major does not arrest a mere translator. An officer of his rank would collar a prince or a baron.

"Where is Prince Antonio?"

"On a trip to Lisbon. He should be back in three or four weeks."

Major Baumeister threw the papers to the floor and nodded to his soldiers to follow him. Just before stepping out the door, he said to Jean de Dieu in a tone dripping with contempt, "Tell Prince Antonio he is summoned to the Hôtel Majestic as soon as he returns. Don't make me come back here. This place reeks of diamond smuggling."

The major was sure the prince would rush back and offer him a bribe to allow him to continue his operation. The Hôtel Majestic, on Avenue Kléber, was the headquarters of the Nazi high command. Suspects who entered there did not always come out alive.

Jean de Dieu knew he had to contact his employer as soon as possible. There was going to be a showdown.

Major F. Baumeister

The major was a member of the Nazi intelligence service, the Sicherheitsdienst, commonly known as the SD. He had obtained the post in Paris as a result of his long-standing career as an opportunist. A native of Hamburg, he had joined the Nazi organization in its early days, in the thirties, and had steadily climbed up through the ranks.

He had begun with brawls with Communists in the smoky bars of Hamburg, and then he had taken part in the harassment and arrests of intellectuals opposed to Nazism in Berlin. His master stroke had been his role in the annexation of Austria in 1938. He had organized clandestine operations, acts of sabotage, and assassinations of Austrian adversaries in order to consolidate the Anschluss. He had also taken part in the invasion of Poland in September 1939. He had trained elite killers recruited from Polish and Slovak gangs. He had even trafficked in gold and diamonds stolen from Jews for the benefit of his superiors.

Baumeister had been sent to Paris because of his command of the French language. He had learned it from his mother, a stern, cold woman who taught in a private school. In addition, he knew how to crush urban pockets of resistance and he extracted information with the patience of a true sadist. With the resistance becoming better organized, a torturer of Baumeister's calibre was needed.

Baumeister was back on the fourth floor of the Hôtel Majestic. His office, spacious and richly furnished, reflected his success. He couldn't afford to mess up. No longer a young officer, he wouldn't be given a second chance. Facing him on his desk was a photo of his daughter with her husband in uniform. She had married a young soldier who was fighting on the Eastern Front. The major had put the photo there to create an image of himself as a respectable family man. His wife and daughter knew nothing of his activities as a torturer. They thought he was an administrator.

In front of him were three stacks of files that his secretary, Magda, had put there for him before leaving. The yellow stack, on the left, consisted of cases that needed to be verified, the brown stack was of promising cases, and the third stack, the red one, the tallest, was of arrests and results of interrogations.

Prince Antonio's case had arisen from a tip-off by a neighbor on his floor, Simon Giraudoux, who sold alcohol illegally to Paris restaurants. Business was booming and he could afford a classy apartment in an affluent neighbourhood. The case had ended up at the police station of his arrondissement. Simon, who called himself Pastis, had quickly confessed after being hung by his feet for several minutes. The major had noted that police methods for getting a suspect to talk had advanced under the Occupation. To avoid prison, the man had ratted on his neighbour, the African prince. He had described him as a fake student, always smartly dressed, whose name was Antonio. He said he was visited at all hours of the night by men in suits with briefcases. That fake student didn't speak a word of French, he was barely able to exchange basic greetings with neighbours. Pastis had added that the neighbour travelled around Paris with a translator and a driver.

Thanks to this tip-off, Pastis was only fined 200 francs, and all the bottles of alcohol he was storing in a warehouse in the Paris suburbs were confiscated.

The police officers had created a file on Prince Antonio, which they labelled "Black Diamonds." They suspected him of espionage and believed he was only pretending to be an African prince. The judicial police had transferred the investigation to the Nazi intelligence service, the Gestapo. This was a case that merited the particular skills of the German experts. Since the investigation had been opened, Prince Antonio's file had been in the stack requiring verification. He had been identified as a student at the Institut d'Ethnologie. The Gestapo had shown up at the institute and demanded a report on him. The Black student was brilliant, according to the professors' notes. They had described a tall, thin man with a haughty bearing who did not come to class regularly although he always handed in his assignments on time.

That was why Major Baumeister had concluded, upon entering the apartment, that it was the Black prince who stood before him. However, the man had denied it and, when interrogated, had shown Portuguese identification papers. Yet he had spoken German without the least hint of a Portuguese accent. This fact greatly intrigued the major, and Jean de Dieu had thus escaped being hauled in. The major preferred to use him as bait. The translator would alert his employer, who would be forced to buy his employee's freedom in exchange for precious stones. That at least was the major's thinking. He assumed that these Blacks descended from apes could easily be held to ransom. He would be rich in a few weeks while hardly breaking a sweat. Who said crime doesn't pay? Not a Nazi.

But Baumeister knew he had to tread carefully. The prince was a national of a neutral country, Portugal. An African under the protection of the Portuguese authorities. With a few calls to secret agents in Lisbon, he learned that Prince Antonio had some well-placed friends in the Portuguese customs service and the Salazar government. The Black man was untouchable in Lisbon. Things had to be done properly. Otherwise, the people in Lisbon who benefited from the African's largesse by closing their eyes to his illegal imports would cry bloody murder and hold Baumeister accountable. The major preferred to avoid embarrassing his superiors and ending up on a battlefield in Libya helping incompetent Italian soldiers. So he ordered that the Black prince's telephone be bugged and a tail be put on his translator to find out when the prince would return. Baumeister would arrest him personally in order to maintain control of the situation and pocket his precious stones.

Baumeister moved the Prince Antonio file to the brown stack; it now looked promising. This put him in a good mood. Recently there had been nothing in the red stack but prisoners who would rather die under torture than talk. The attacks on rail transport, the sabotage of power lines, and the killings of isolated German soldiers had begun to sap the major's morale. These incidents had occurred at Chalon-sur-Saône, Bourg-en-Bresse, Grenoble, and the list went on and on. The resistance fighters, in organized gangs, seemed willing and ready to die as martyrs. Of course, the collaborationist newspapers never reported these incidents, and one of the major's tasks was to make sure that continued to be the case. The French must above all not be allowed to dream of eventual liberation. They had to supply the German Empire with coal and manpower for the arms factories. Nazi Germany was expecting locomotives and trucks as well as draft horses for agriculture.

Jean de Dieu Gets to Work

The translator left his boss's apartment about fifteen minutes after Baumeister and his men. He took care to lose possible tails by following a circuitous route. After Châtelet-les-Halles, he walked towards Rue Pierre-Lescot, then took Rue des Innocents and Rue de la Ferronnerie, and then zigzagged to Rambuteau métro station, where he disappeared into the bowels of the earth. He had to get in contact with Prince Antonio. Sitting in a photo booth, he took a picture of himself while waiting for the train to start. He hated that swelling on his mouth. But Baumeister would have to wait. Jean de Dieu promised himself he would have his revenge. He quickly exited the photo booth just as the doors of the train were about to close.

He went to his Brazilian friend Armando Luis Pereira's café, on Rue Champollion in the 5th arrondissement, which was called Le Croissant Doré. It was swarming with students reviewing their lessons over cooling cups of coffee or quietly bemoaning their lack of freedom to their friends. There was no doubt the Nazis had informants here, but the Brazilian played Maurice Chevalier, Suzy Solidor, or even Édith Piaf very loud to make it hard to overhear conversations.

Prince Antonio had helped finance the purchase of the café, using cash so that no one at the bank knew they were connected. Armando, a forty-year-old musician, had tried his luck playing in the cabarets of Paris in the thirties, without success. He had fallen in love with a Frenchwoman before the war and settled there for good. He had met her when he was playing the samba on a guitar one summer on Rue Dauphine. As for the prince, their paths had crossed at a Brazilian music show. Armando was the prince's go-between with his employees when he was away from France.

Jean de Dieu went in and ordered a carafe of wine. When Armando brought it to him, he paid for it immediately, with a coded message for the prince hidden between the bank notes. Armando went to the telephone in the back of the establishment, dialed the operator, and gave her a Lisbon phone number. She asked him to wait while she connected him. Armando heard a click and a familiar deep voice said in Portuguese, "Hello?"

"May I speak to Matheus Gomes, please?"

"There's no one by that name here, I'm sorry."

Armando hung up, satisfied that he had done his part, as simple as it was. He had recognized the voice of his friend Prince Antonio at the other end of the line. The prince had received the call in the luxurious apartment he rented permanently in Lisbon, not far from Praça do Comércio Square, in the Baixa neighbourhood.

The message came as a shock to the prince and he had to sit down to regain his composure. Its meaning was clear: "Do not come back to Paris for the time being, something isn't right." But what? He went over to the bay window that looked out on red tile roofs. He could see the equestrian statue of King José I of Portugal. He imagined himself, like the king, on his galloping steed, trampling snakes.

His Highness finally calmed down and took a philosophical view of the situation. He would go to the port of Lisbon to accept the coffee shipment from his father, King Pedro VII. He would bribe the customs agents, remove the diamonds in their special little bags, and send the coffee on to the finest hotels in the Portuguese capital. Then he would forward the profits to the king. All in all, that would easily take four weeks if he did things at a leisurely pace, until the year-end holidays. Then he would have to make a decision. Whether to return to Paris or have his two associates come and join him in Lisbon.

But there was still the problem of the diamonds. He possessed some very beautiful, extremely desirable stones. He had always returned to Lisbon before selling all his merchandise so as never to be short of the precious stones. He kept them in the apartment in Paris. If the Nazis got their hands on them, he would lose a fortune. He understood that an officer was waiting to hold him to ransom. Otherwise, the Germans would already have searched his apartment. There must be someone who wanted a cut over the long term. Of course, it was out of the question that Prince Antonio give in to them. The diamonds would have to be moved.

Things hadn't reached that point yet. From his window, he watched thousands of *refugiados* lined up in the winter rain in front of the wickets of the central post office, near a large square. Those refugees were trying to obtain visas for other places far from the Nazis and persecution. There were Jews, but also Poles, Czechs, Frenchmen, all of them hunted and exhausted. He imagined the questions the customs agents were asking, what they would require to allow them to escape. How had these people gotten out of the countries they had crossed to reach Portugal? Did they have transit visas for Lisbon? Did they know anyone in the United States? In Argentina? Could they produce tickets for the plane or ship? A multitude of questions like daggers in the backs of the weary fugitives.

Prince Antonio felt a twinge of sadness. Sarah. That name was always with him. However, in Paris, there were Isabelle, Nathalie, and even a Fatou, who had sweetened his nights in the apartment in La Muette. But Sarah, that little brunette who had dyed her hair blond to look less Jewish, forever had a special place in his heart. She had given him a beautiful little baby, who was now a toddler. That proof of love in time of war moved him deeply. If the Nazis learned of their existence, they would blackmail him. He thought about how to keep them out of harm's way. Before that phone call, he had been sure he was protecting them. Now, he knew he could lose them.

Sarah lived in a discreet apartment in the 19th arrondissement, not far from the slaughterhouses of La Villette. She was a Pole, Sarah Lazowski, nicknamed Suzy. She had fled Poland after the German invasion in 1939 and worked in a hairdressing salon on Rue de Rennes. He spoke no French, she spoke no Portuguese. But it had only taken a few words in rudimentary English to light a spark between them. It happened in a métro station. A request for information, an exchange of glances. She had understood that he wanted to see her again. He was a handsome man, dignified and elegant. He hadn't pushed things, he had waited patiently several weeks for her to give herself to him one summer night. She suspected that Antonio was seeing other women. But she knew they shared a genuine love. In these times of war, Suzy felt, that was already a lot. She lived without being sure of the future.

Prince Antonio looked out at the Tagus River on the edge of Praça do Comércio, flowing towards the Atlantic Ocean. He promised himself he would get Sarah and his little Rodolfo out as soon as possible.

All Cats Are Grey in the Dark

Jean de Dieu was pacing up and down on Rue Saint-Georges, in the 9th arrondissement. He had been there since nightfall a half-hour ago, waiting for someone. Well-off Parisians were hurrying to the cinema or going to cafés for a glass of wine with friends. And then there were those who, suitcases in hand, were looking for a place to live after the bombings by the Royal Air Force. The night was another world, a world of rich, high-rolling aristocrats, destitute Communists, people who slashed the tires of dignitaries' Mercedes, starving people and beggars, victims of the food rationing imposed by the occupying forces. The cold was making the Parisians hurry. The German soldiers, on the other hand, well fed and bundled up, were strolling around in groups and going to entertainment venues.

Jean de Dieu went into a café to warm up. His fedora pulled down and slightly tilted, he smoked a Gitane while waiting for Jenny, a lady friend who worked nearby. His glass of Raynal cognac stood untouched on the table of the café, which was not far from the brothel called Le Chat Botté, or Puss in Boots. He was pretending to read *La Gerbe*, a fascist newspaper with a front page story about the arrest of some resistance fighters who were about to blow up trucks supplying the German military. In reality, Jean de Dieu was trying to pick up snatches of the conversation around him in order to know whether he would have to leave the place quickly. What was his friend Jenny doing?

Jenny worked at the Chat Botté and was one of its main attractions. An Asian girl, with long, silky, jet-black hair, almond eyes, and an enigmatic smile. He had met her through Hans, who offered his services as a driver to some of the ladies of the night who lived on the other side of the city. He used Prince Antonio's car and made a lot of money. The fuel shortage was becoming increasingly acute and few drivers ventured out at night. Hans had once told Jenny that she reminded him of his friend Jean de Dieu. "In what way?" she had asked. "You look like someone who isn't afraid of anything or anyone," he had replied. She had smiled and, bringing a match to her cigarette in its holder, said, "I can tell who my enemies are. I sleep with them." When Hans recounted this to him, Jean de Dieu had wanted to meet her and recruit her. Knowing what the Nazis were planning to do could be useful for a smuggler.

Jenny entered the café and came over to Jean de Dieu. She was made up like a goddess of the night and dressed in a black coat with a faux fur collar. Her face spoke volumes. She was not happy. She sat down across from him after smiling at Roger, the owner, behind the counter, who would bring her current favourite drink, mulled wine sprinkled with cinnamon. She opened her hand; it held a small mirror that she used to check out the café patrons. "You know I'm busy this time of day."

"It was urgent," answered Jean de Dieu without taking his eyes off the newspaper.

"I turn three tricks a day, that makes eighteen tricks in six days. I'll have fewer this week, because of you."

The African smiled, a touch of reproach in his eyes. He knew Jenny well. She always liked to remind him what she did for a living. She did it to provoke him, to get him to reveal his feelings about it. He never made any comment.

"You know that if I'm taking the risk of seeing you at work and not at your place, it's because there's a problem."

She listened, concerned.

He lowered his voice. "I had a visit from a Boche. A certain Major F. Baumeister. Does that ring any bells?"

She pretended to be thinking. "No. But I see he left you a souvenir," she added, indicating his lower lip. She took a handkerchief out of her coat pocket and applied it to his lip.

Jean de Dieu put up with this for a few seconds, grimacing. Then he pulled back his head and said, "It's okay, I'll survive."

Annoyed, she put away her handkerchief and crossed her arms, waiting.

"From now on, don't call the prince's apartment. And don't go there. The place is definitely being watched. If you have any information for me, go through Hans."

"Did they arrest the prince?"

"No. He's in Lisbon. But they mistook me for him."

He gestured towards the newspaper on the table. "I left something for you."

"Thank you." Jenny smiled at him for the first time since she had arrived.

He realized he had been waiting for this moment. He liked seeing the whiteness of her teeth. "I have a favour to ask you. Can you find out about Baumeister's activities outside the office? About his private life, at night?"

That was Jenny's speciality. She had worked in several brothels. The Occupation was profitable for her. The German soldiers and the middle-class collaborators were thirsty for exoticism. There were the beautiful Black women who did contortions for them like Josephine Baker, and then there were the Indian and Chinese women. The exoticism of women from far-off lands was worth its weight in gold.

"Okay. But I can't promise anything. The girls are more and more scared. The soldiers are nervous and there's not as much pillow talk anymore."

"Do your best. I need to know that officer's little secrets. He owes me something."

Jenny looked again at his lower lip. "Ask Lola to take care of that."

She noted his slight frown.

"It's all over with Lola."

Jean de Dieu had happened to cross paths with Jenny when he had a conquest on his arm, a florist from Rue Dauphine called Lola, a brunette, tall as a giraffe and rather heavy-hipped. He had had to introduce them. It had been easy come, easy go with Lola, but Jenny hadn't forgotten her.

"Yes, it's over with her. She asked too many questions. Like you."

Annoyed again, she picked up the newspaper and got up to leave. "I was going to give you a kiss, but I don't feel like it anymore."

She turned on her heel and joined the pedestrians outside the café. Jean de Dieu regretted his last comment. In fact, Lola had gone away without giving him an address. That was life under the Occupation. Barely known, already forgotten.

He would have liked a kiss from Jenny.

He finished his cognac and headed home. The hour was late and there weren't many night owls. Identity checks were becoming more frequent. He showed his papers to two police officers on bicycle, their capes flapping in the wind. He had to make sure once again that he was not being followed. He slipped into the shadow of a carriage entrance along the way and listened to the footsteps and conversations of the passersby. They were people in a hurry to get home. There was no danger.

He arrived at Rue Grégoire-de-Tours. He lived at the south end of the street. Once inside the building, he pressed the button for the elevator but didn't take it. He climbed the stairs silently in order to check if there was anyone waiting for him at the door to the apartment. There was no one. Once inside, he made himself comfortable in front of his coal stove and took a book on the history of the Germanic peoples from his well-stocked bookcase.

Jenny, the Chinese Woman from Far Away

If she were asked what exoticism was, Jenny would answer, "It's what pays my rent." She didn't think there was anything special about her almond eyes and her slender body with its firm curves. She had left a country full of women like her in the late 1930s. But in Paris, she knew, she was rare and desirable. Born in northern China not far from the border with the Soviet Union, Jenny had at the age of fifteen made a decision to seduce in order to escape. She tried to get to Hong Kong, but did not succeed. Then she went to Macao on the arm of a Portuguese colonial administrator who had been looking for a servant and found a lover. Called back to Lisbon, the administrator took Jenny with him. She left him the first chance she got. Too old and already married. Back then, she called herself Cherry. Her real name was Lee Hong Ma, but you wouldn't get very far in the seduction game in the West with a name like that.

She had decided to leave Lisbon and try her luck in Paris after seeing the City of Lights in a movie. She didn't know how to dance, but she did know how to attract men. Narrow-waisted and alluring, she smoked menthol cigarettes with languid elegance and dreamed of landing a role in a movie. That was all it took for her to make the trip. In 1938, Spain was consumed by civil war. Jenny knew that getting to Paris as a woman on her own would take courage and nerves of steel. On her stopover in Barcelona, which was still in the Republicans' hands, she was interrogated by the anarchist and anti-fascist forces.

She had waited in line clutching her papers as a Portuguese citizen born in Macao. Her ex-lover, who had no hard feelings, had made sure she was provided with those documents and an exit visa. The person in front of her in the line, who was barely thirty years old, had not been able to convince the interrogator. He ended up lying in a thicket not far away with two bullets in his head.

She had kept her cool throughout an interrogation about her Chinese origins. The soldiers at first suspected her of being a spy for Mao, but her disdain for the Maoists was genuine. She got to Paris safe and sound.

The German invasion caught her off guard. The invasion of Poland in 1939 had been dramatic, but when the Wehrmacht turned towards western Europe and in May 1940 occupied Luxembourg, the Netherlands, and Belgium, Jenny realized that the Germans would take Paris. She was getting ready to return to Lisbon when she heard German boots marching into Paris. Something happened within her when she saw the city she had fallen in love with sullied by the presence of those soldiers.

Jenny, the independent woman, the one who had promised herself freedom as an adolescent in her native China, was not going to give in. She had managed to survive the Chinese armed gangs that controlled the opium trade, and she was not going to submit to a bunch of fanatics who saluted each other like Roman statues.

Now there was this African man who had been occupying her thoughts for the last year. She had known as soon as she laid eyes on Jean de Dieu that he would steal her heart. Hans had stopped at his place and introduced them one day while driving her home. She had seen a slender man with a pleasant smile and discovered he could charm her without seeming to try. He had made small talk in a French that you couldn't quite place.

Jenny had fallen in love only once before. His name was Jian and he was an aspiring swing singer. Their affair had started when he was a backup singer in Macao. Then he had lost himself to opium. Little by little, he had turned into a pimp. He had sold her to his friends for the drug he was hooked on. The opium had stolen him from Jenny.

Her heartache had eventually abated. But to avoid ever being burned again, she'd decided to appeal to men's vices instead of their hearts. In that she reigned as absolute mistress. She never gave herself completely, and thus kept herself armed against getting burned or betrayed with broken promises.

However, this African had found a way into her dreams and desires. How could she tell him that without driving him away? What was the love of a prostitute worth? Sometimes, she managed to forget her fascination with him by taking a lover, one of the young men attracted by her exoticism, but that would only last a few months before she found herself once again under Jean de Dieu's spell. He had never made disrespectful comments about her profession. Whenever he visited her at work, the other women noticed that they talked to each other almost like a couple. Although Jenny said they were just friends, they didn't believe it. "When you spend your time satisfying people's urges, you know how to recognize true feelings," her perceptive neighbour, Gigi, had said.

In her apartment, she would often hum Édith Piaf's song "L'accordéoniste." It was kind of her own story, and she knew it.

The working girl is pretty
At her streetcorner spot
She gives her many clients
All the joy they've bought
When the job is over
She goes along her way
To dream of a better day.

Hans and the Prince's Apartment

Hans had gone out in his new suit. He left the Ménil Palace, a neighbourhood movie theatre where he had watched *L'héritier des Mondésir* [*The Mondesir Heir*], a comedy that had just gone into general release. He would have had to pay twice as much for its first run. He took the métro to Prince Antonio's apartment, where he was planning to drink a nice glass of whisky with Jean de Dieu. He didn't know that his friend had received a visit from the Gestapo and was not there anymore.

He walked quickly through the night city. His steady footsteps rang out in the dark alleys. On the alert for the slightest suspicious sound, he noticed the glowing golden eyes of the alley cats that were fighting and howling. There were more and more Wehrmacht soldiers in the streets. He avoided a checkpoint on the way to the apartment by swerving to take a different route. The soldiers there were harassing a drunk and didn't notice him. And the light from the streetlamps was dim. They had been blackened to make things harder for the bombers of the Royal Air Force.

He glanced up at the apartment from the sidewalk across the street. Something wasn't right. Everything was dark. Usually, there was a glow in the prince's bedroom window. The apartment seemed empty. Hans checked the cars parked in front of the building. Nobody in them. He decided to go upstairs to see if Jean de Dieu had fallen asleep and simply forgotten to leave his bedside lamp on. He had the key to the ground floor. As soon as he unlocked the door, he regretted his haste. Two heads popped up in one of the cars parked across the street. He closed the door again without entering the building, kicking himself for falling into the trap. Two men, in plain dark suits quickly got out of the car. He sensed they were Gestapo.

"Police! Halt!" shouted a French voice.

He did not comply. He disappeared around the corner of the street.

"Police! Don't move or I'll shoot," shouted the other policeman.

Hans had slipped into the darkness of a narrow street. He raced along, already holding his ivory-grip Luger. The first policeman stumbled on the cobblestones in the dark, and the other one helped him up before continuing the pursuit. That fall was a lucky break for Hans. He reached the prince's car.

The two policemen continued, each on one side of the line of cars parked on the street. The sound of footsteps had stopped and they wondered where the suspect could be hiding. They methodically checked under and inside the vehicles. They got to the end of the little street and looked at each other, bewildered. Where could that Black have run off to? One of them thought of a manhole, but the guy would never have had time to lift the heavy metal cover and slip into it. "Merde!" spat the other one, furious. He was already imagining the tongue-lashing they'd get from their superior. It was the headquarters on Rue Kléber that had ordered the surveillance of the building. Was all that waiting for nothing? No, that Black couldn't be far away. Maybe in a car, but which one? They had already looked, but perhaps too quickly.

"Did you see what he looked like?" asked his partner.

"No. Black on black."

They weren't aware that Hans was listening, holding his breath. They were still scratching their heads, baffled, and one of them had started thinking of the best lie to tell their boss. The other, more astute, realized that the suspect could be watching them. Opening car doors could prove fatal. He kept his weapon in his hand, while his partner had holstered his.

In the darkness, they hadn't noticed that the driver's door of one of the cars was slightly ajar. Hans was hiding in the beige Renault. Fortunately, he still had the keys. He'd had the presence of mind to turn off the ceiling light before hiding in it. One of the men took another look inside. He didn't see anything move. Hans fired at him through the rear window. A shot to his head that immediately sent him sprawling to the ground to the sound of breaking glass.

The other one froze and regretted putting his weapon back in the holster under his armpit. He raised his hands without turning around. "Wait, don't shoot. It was a routine check. We can talk," he said in a tone that didn't sound very convincing.

Hans didn't answer. The area would be swarming with police in a matter of minutes.

The Gestapo man turned quickly, his hand reaching under his coat. He didn't have time to draw before Hans shot him in the chest, again through the rear window. He collapsed onto his back and his eyes closed.

Hans got out of the vehicle, put away his weapon, and glanced at the windows of the surrounding apartments. He didn't see anyone, but that didn't mean anything. Since the Occupation, Paris was a hotbed of informers and opportunists of all kinds. He was sure that unknown individuals would steal the policemen's automatic pistols before backup arrived. Before leaving, he checked the coat of the second policeman. His identity card showed he was indeed a member of the French Gestapo of Rue Lauriston, also known as the *Carlingue*. Hans knew that if he were picked up by them, he would never come out alive.

He started the Renault and headed towards Créteil, in the suburbs. The car was his only way to get out of the area. He knew the streets of Paris well. When he drove Jenny home, he would keep to the speed limit and show both their papers to the police. He would explain that the woman in the back was the mistress of a German officer at Hôtel Crillon. That was the headquarters of the military governor of Paris. They would let him pass without further questioning.

Hans crossed paths with officers on bicycle who whistled for him to stop, but he ignored them. The description of the vehicle would be known in a few hours and he had to get to his destination before the whole of Paris was looking for it. He reached the southeast suburbs in ten minutes and turned onto Rue Chéret, then stopped on the left at Rue du Cap. He got out, leaving the motor running, and knocked on the window of a little house with a garage. A Black man peeked out the window. The garage doors opened, and two other Black men motioned to guide the Renault in. When the doors were closed, silence returned to the suburb. The three men watched Hans get out of the car.

Once inside, the men sat down around a table with a deck of cards, glasses, and a big half-full bottle of American whisky on it. Happy to be safe, Hans burst out laughing.

His friend Mathias Bombo, a musician from Cameroon, told him in German to keep quiet, a smile on his lips. "You'll wake up the whole neighbourhood."

Hans hugged Mathias, whose nickname was Matty. He did the same with Jean Monséjour and Sylvestre Dubonnet, who were both Martinican musicians.

He had met Matty when he was playing guitar at La Cigale, in Montmartre. He had brought one of the ladies of the night there and was hoping to find another woman looking for a driver. Matty was on the stage as part of the Quintette du Hot Club de France, replacing a guitarist who played with Django Reinhardt. Hans couldn't believe his eyes. A Black man playing on the same stage with Reinhardt! It was a total shock. He stayed behind to talk to him during the break. The man had a German accent. He was a Cameroonian who had experienced German colonization before the Treaty of Versailles turned his country into a French colony. They had immediately become friends. Matty repaired cars to make ends meet. Hans regularly brought Prince Antonio's Renault to his place.

"How's it going, fellas?" Hans asked his friends.

The three were all talking at once. Hans acted as if it didn't bother him. It was a habit he didn't understand. But he got right to the point. "I need you to make this pretty gal disappear," he said, indicating the car. "New rear window, new paint job, black. New tires."

"Are you crazy? There aren't any new tires in the whole country! At least not in the occupied zone," said Jean in a hoarse voice. He was a double bass player, tall and stout with laughing eyes.

"We can replace the spoked rims with twelve-hole rims," said Sylvestre, a jazz drummer, always ready to compromise.

“Yeah, good idea,” said Matty. “That’ll make it look different.”

“I want you to cover the steering wheel with velvet and remove the chrome from the headlights,” specified Hans. “Oh, yes. And convert it to charcoal.”

“We don’t know how to do that.”

“Find someone.”

“It will cost you a pretty penny,” said Matty.

“The prince always pays his bills.”

“Then it’s as good as done,” said Jean.

“Have a drink, we’re about to finish this game. You can start the next one with us,” said Matty.

Hans sat down and Sylvestre handed him a glass.

“Oh yeah. I’ll also need another licence plate.”

The three men laughed but made sure to put their hands over their mouths to avoid making too much noise.

“Of course, brother!”

Matty slapped him on the back and Sylvestre motioned them to be quiet. The card game was starting again.

The Major Is Not Happy

Major Baumeister was drumming his fingers nervously on his desk while waiting for his lieutenant, Lukas Betz, to arrive. Betz was five minutes late, which was unacceptable. Yet the day had started well. He had woken up in his beautiful apartment on Rue Dufrenoy, in the 16th arrondissement, which belonged to a well-to-do Parisian exiled in New York City. He had had breakfast with his current mistress, Angèle, whom he had met at the Sphinx, a high-class brothel. The evening before, they had gone to see the German movie *Brand im Ozean* [Fire on the ocean] at the Gaumont Palace near Place de Clichy.

This morning, Hermann, his driver, had dropped him at the Hôtel Majestic, where his secretary, Magda, had served him a black coffee with two spoonfuls of sugar. It was real coffee, not chicory. The sugar came from Germany, it was not an ersatz sweetener like saccharine. Nothing fake for the masters of the world.

While waiting for his subordinate, he leafed through the coloured file folders his secretary had laid out on his desk. He was not interested in either the yellow or the brown stack. Those two required verification and he was thinking only of results. He began with the red stack. Several arrests in recent weeks, and many confessions. Some people in the resistance had played the hero, but they ended up six feet under. Once he was finished with the red stack, the major started on the brown stack. He read a report from the *Carlingue* regarding the address in La Muette that was under surveillance. This ruined his morning. Two officers killed by a Black, according to a witness. He was in such a rage that he didn't even look at the third stack, the yellow one. His blood boiling, he called Magda. "Come here right now!"

Magda, a young blond woman, hurried into his office. "Yes, Major?"

"What's Lieutenant Betz doing?"

Just then, Betz rushed into the office and gave the Nazi salute, clicking his heels. "Heil Hitler!" he exclaimed, out of breath.

The major returned the salute much less emphatically.

"Apologies, Major. Saboteurs slashed the tires of our bus. I had to commandeer a bicycle. The cyclist was not happy, I had to use force. So that's it. I promise you it won't happen again."

Suddenly the incident of the murdered members of the French Gestapo could wait a few moments.

"Is the cyclist dead?"

"No, but he'll need a few stitches."

The major stood up and gave Betz a satisfied smile. "I like stories with happy endings. You're forgiven for the delay... this time,"

He took his monocle out of an inside pocket and rubbed it with a white handkerchief pulled from his well-pressed uniform.

"Frau Magdalena, bring Lieutenant Betz a cup of real coffee to help him recover from the shock."

The secretary, happy not to have to suffer her boss's wrath, obeyed without delay.

The major walked to the window with an almost martial step and peered out through his monocle. He took the lens from his eye, blew on it, and rubbed it again, harder. All his movements seemed calculated and precise. When he had put the monocle back over his right eye, he pointed to the brown file folder that had enraged him. "Read the first page," he said to his lieutenant.

Betz, who was familiar with the "Black diamonds" file, could hardly believe his eyes. He made a comment worthy of a young officer influenced more by ideology than action. "How could those agents have been outsmarted by a subhuman? That Black must have blubbered like a monkey and they took pity on him! You must never show pity to an inferior being. If you do, he'll stab you in the back," he recited pompously.

The major was aware that his subordinate knew *Mein Kampf* by heart and that he had only one aspiration, to please his superior and rise in the ranks. He was the son of a Hamburg banker who had been one of the first financiers to support the National Socialist Party. Lieutenant Betz was never going to see a battlefield. He knew nothing of combat. The major made fun of him behind his back. In his eyes, Betz was nothing but a spoiled child.

"Contact Rue Lauriston and tell them that from now on we'll take care of surveillance on the apartment in the 16th. Then find out from our informants in Lisbon when the Black prince is supposed to return. I'm eager to interrogate him."

Lukas Betz left immediately to carry out his orders.

Baumeister was swamped with work as 1941 drew to a close. Attacks and attempted murders of German officers had increased. That meant he was carrying out more interrogations and torture. The Nazis were facing growing problems in the occupied zone. Too many antifascists from Poland, the Netherlands, and Luxembourg were joining with the French ones, attempting to destabilize the occupier. In addition, clandestine leaflets and newspapers were proliferating.

But the major was determined to bring down Prince Antonio. That Black who strutted around dressed to the nines disgusted him. He had seen his type in Austria at the time of the Anschluss. They grew like weeds. They could infect a society with their lewdness if something wasn't done. Some of them played that horrible music called jazz and others knocked up Aryan women.

He had heard about the Battle of Kufra in March 1941, when an army made up mainly of Africans had beaten the Italians and retaken Libya. It was unprecedented. A few hundred Chadians and Cameroonians, probably barefoot, had prevailed over the descendants of ancient Rome. And now there was this so-called prince who was rolling in dough.

In fact, those Blacks were an inferior race and ought to be treated like animals. He was going to make the smuggler hand over all his diamonds, even those he had picked up in Lisbon. He had no intention of delivering the precious gems to his superiors. He was planning to throw that Black in prison and escape by ship to Latin America. The news from the Eastern Front was abysmal and the dismissal of the Commander-in-Chief of the German army, Walther von Brauchitsch, in December had convinced him that it was time to disappear. He would leave without his wife and daughter. He wanted a new life. He deserved one after his years of service to the supreme leader, Adolf Hitler.

The lieutenant came back into his office, looking uncomfortable. Something was troubling him. "What if the African decided to stay in Lisbon for good?"

"Paris is the goose that lays him golden eggs," said the major with a malicious smile. "He'll be back."

"Maybe we should search his apartment? His diamonds could be there," the lieutenant suggested, fear in his eyes.

The major drummed his fingers on the table, annoyed. "What did they teach you in school about investigation? If I order a search, he won't come back! I want him to return for his loot. He has to think he can negotiate. Then, once we've got our hands on him, we'll be able to dismantle his whole network!"

Lukas Betz pretended to understand. He was not very convinced, but he didn't dare antagonize his superior.

Baumeister wanted not only the prince's precious gems but also his life. The man had the impertinence to live like a pasha among the German conquerors. He'd have to pay for it. The major believed that these primitive people were easily overcome by emotion, that they attached little importance to cold, hard reason. The prince would panic when he learned he was wanted by the Germans, and would come running back to save his business.

"Find me the translator. You know? That arrogant fellow who took a bath at his boss's place. Prince Antonio could return to Paris just to try to save his translator."

"João de Deus Kassoma?"

Lieutenant Betz had read the name in the "Black diamonds" file earlier and wanted to impress his boss. The major gave him an icy stare. "Do you actually think that's his real name? You were present in the prince's apartment when he was questioned. Did you not notice he didn't have the slightest Portuguese accent? Do I need to draw you a picture, Lieutenant? There's something shady about that man."

"You're right, Major," Betz acknowledged.

"Get a composite sketch done of the Black who killed the two Frenchmen on Rue Lauriston. And that translator must go to libraries and cafés where intellectuals gather. The way he spoke gave him away. Go to the Sorbonne and the Latin Quarter, ask around. Someone must know his real name. And then..."

"Yes?"

"When you talk to the men at Rue Lauriston, tell them the order to put the prince's apartment under surveillance comes from high up, very high up, at the Hôtel Majestic. Those frogs will understand. Above all, you mustn't offend them. We need those flunkies to cleanse the city of Jews and other riffraff.

"You can count on me, Major."

The lieutenant gave another Nazi salute, clicking his heels, and Baumeister returned the salute, hoping that one day a resistance fighter would blow out the brains of this spoiled brat in a Paris alley. He hated idealists.

Strategy and Preparations

It was two weeks since Hans had killed the police officers. Jean de Dieu had phoned him at his place the day after the shootings and Hans had given him a report in the original argot he used, German and French with the addition of expressions in Swahili that Jean de Dieu had taught him. The prince's right-hand man had ordered Hans to keep a low profile. They had to avoid attracting the attention of the authorities. They had to wait for orders from Prince Antonio, who was still in Lisbon, and who had managed to sell most of his father's coffee to Portuguese buyers who were not very particular about the provenance of the merchandise.

Jean de Dieu and Hans were in the back room of Le Croissant Doré on Rue Champollion. Armando had summoned them to the café to receive Prince Antonio's instructions. He had gotten a letter from Lisbon the day before.

On the little kitchen table was a handwritten sheet of paper. It was officially addressed to Armando Luis Pereira. Armando carefully unfolded it. He pointed to the iron that was close at hand. "This letter needed quite a lot of ironing."

The two friends understood immediately that the letter had been written in invisible ink. To an unsuspecting person, it would look as if Prince Antonio had sent a completely innocuous message to Armando.

The letter had made the journey with a man who was taking up a post in Paris as an attaché at the Portuguese embassy. He had carried it in a diplomatic pouch, which, according to international convention, could not be searched. On the brown envelope was Armando's name and the address of Le Croissant Doré. Once the letter reached Paris, the driver from the embassy had passed it to the café owner in a newspaper over a cup of Brazilian coffee.

In the writing that was visible, the prince spoke in Portuguese about his health and his monotonous life in Lisbon. But between the lines, he had used an ink made of baking soda mixed with water, which was invisible to the naked eye, and writing with a cotton swab in Swahili, had given his instructions. To reveal those words, one had to apply heat to the letter.

Armando had started with steam from a pot of water boiling on the coal stove. The words had begun to appear. To make them completely readable, he had used the iron, although he knew he was running the risk of burning the paper. Little by little, the message had become visible. He was proud of his work.

Jean de Dieu had come with Hans less than twenty-four hours after hearing from Armando. He took the letter and began translating it into French to read to his comrades. He intended to burn it immediately after reading it.

These recent weeks had been a game of cat-and-mouse for him and Hans. They often went to public places to talk in order to throw the Germans off their scent. Jean de Dieu visited public libraries and borrowed books on ethnology. He had developed an interest in the field. That was just as well, because he realized he would have to continue playing the role of student prince. The German soldiers still didn't know his actual identity. As for going back to his place, that would take time. The apartment was rented in the name of a former girlfriend who had decided to go to the Free Zone. But she had kept her name on the lease to avoid being questioned by the Nazi authorities about where she was going and why. The concierge, fearing problems with the police, had preferred to look the other way and pretend that the young woman would come back. In any case, the Black man always added an extra fifty francs to the rent money. Who would complain about such generosity? Not the concierge, who pocketed the difference.

Hans had almost no money left. He was renting a room in a shabby hotel in the suburbs and the frequent train trips and the detours required to make sure he wasn't followed were draining his funds.

Jean de Dieu finished translating the message into French. He read it:

> *Dear brothers and friends,*
>
> *Thank you for keeping me up to date on the latest events. I am very grateful for your courage and your collective efforts. I have two urgent requests. The first one is that you retrieve the remaining stones from my apartment, which they must be watching. Jean de Dieu knows where the stones are. Sell them, make them disappear. The second request is that you empty the safe. I give you permission to use those funds. Know that I intend to come back to Paris. For that to be possible, any damaging evidence has to disappear.*
>
> *I will let you know when I will return. It's a matter of weeks. If any of you has to leave Paris or France, make sure Jean de Dieu is able to contact you.*
>
> *Good luck.*

Prince Antonio had added his family coat of arms as a signature. Jean de Dieu memorized the Swahili message before burning everything.

Actually, the letter contained an additional paragraph that the translator did not read out loud, as a precaution. In it, Prince Antonio spoke of Suzy Lazowski, a Polish Jew living near La Villette. He was counting on Jean de Dieu to get her out of the country. There was also a child, barely two years old, whose name was Rodolfo. That said it all. Prince Antonio did not need to beg or insist. He knew that the translator would do everything he could to get them to Lisbon.

Hans was about to say something when the café owner gestured to him to be quiet. He heard loud voices in the front. His customers were generally quieter. Without waiting, Armando opened the door to the bar and the two friends heard him say, "Welcome to Le Croissant Doré. What can I get you?"

The man with the loudest voice answered, "Police. Are you naturalized?" and showed a French Gestapo card.

"Yes, Monsieur. My wife is Parisian."

"Where does she come from exactly?"

"Nadège? Rue des Lombards. Born and raised on that street."

"You got kids?" asked the other voice, not quite as loud.

"No, unfortunately. The Good Lord decided otherwise."

They heard the sound of footsteps and the front door chime. Customers leaving, one after the other, sensing trouble.

"There go your customers. Are you a Communist?" asked the belligerent one.

"Oh, no! In Brazil, we don't even know what that is."

Hans had taken out his 9 mm ivory-grip Luger and had positioned himself behind the door, ready to fire at the first person who dared cross the threshold. Jean de Dieu, too, had come armed, and had drawn his black Ruby from his ankle holster. He kept his finger on the trigger and with his left hand signalled to Hans to stay calm.

A secret door at the back of the café led to the little garden of the neighbour, a postal employee and member of the Resistance.

Hans was glancing towards the emergency exit, afraid more policemen would burst in.

"He really takes us for fools," said the less talkative of the two officers. "There are Communists everywhere."

"Even in Brazil," said the blowhard.

"Listen, we already knew you're French through your wife. We wanted to see if you would confirm it. You know what we call people who are naturalized? Half-umbrellas. Try using that in a downpour, you'll have water up to your underpants!"

His partner guffawed. "We didn't come to bother you," he said. "We've already cut into your clientele for today, maybe even for the whole week if we come back tomorrow. Tell us one thing and then we'll go. And I'll tell my colleague not to bug you anymore. You pal around with Blacks?"

"Yes," admitted Armando in a nonchalant tone of voice. "In Brazil, we have lots of Black people, whole villages, cities too. They're the ones who taught me the samba. You see the guitar here, can I play you something?"

He went to pick up the instrument.

The loud officer slammed his fist down on the wooden counter. "Stop playing us for fools or you'll regret it!"

"Sorry," answered Armando meekly. "What do you want to know, exactly?"

"The names of the Blacks that come to your bar," said the hotheaded one.

"I don't ask people for their names, Messieurs. If I did, I wouldn't have any more customers!"

The one who was acting conciliatory laughed. "You love France, right? You love your little wife, Nadège. Am I right?"

"Yes, I adore my wife. And France too."

"You must read the papers," said the strident one. "If you can read French, you must have heard about the law on the denaturalization of new French citizens. No?"

"Yes, but I don't see..."

"You're going to open your big ears that love the samba, and the next time we come, you're going to give us the names of your Black friends."

In the other room, Jean de Dieu was watching Hans. His friend's jaw was clenched, his hand holding the gun tense. "I don't have any special Black friends. They're customers of the café."

"Not our problem," said the bully. The other one took a few steps in the empty café and said, "I must compliment you on your window. The lettering is nice. It would be too bad if vandals damaged it. There are so many petty criminals in Paris these days. It would cost a fortune to replace a window like that, and it doesn't look like you're rolling in dough."

The threat hit home. Armando replied, "I'll do my best."

The calmer one insisted, "No, do better than that. The Germans would already have trashed your café. We're taking pity on you. The

Germans won't. They'll separate you from Nadège. Forever. They don't like the mixing of races."

Armando didn't answer.

The front door chimed and there was silence again. Jean de Dieu immediately put his weapon away and Hans did the same. Armando was swearing in Portuguese, spouting what Hans thought must be the worst insults he knew, and he didn't stop even when Jean de Dieu put his hand on his shoulder to calm him down. Jean de Dieu squeezed Armando's shoulder, looking into his eyes. "You can stop now. They're gone."

The authoritative tone convinced Armando. "Okay." He was sweating, and Hans brought him a glass of water from the faucet in the kitchen.

"Your customers will come back," said Jean de Dieu. "You can't look all pale and sweaty. Pull yourself together. There's nothing to worry about. The next time those men show up, give them the name João de Deus Kassoma."

Armando took a deep breath to stifle his panic. "I'm sorry for the problems I'm causing you. I don't know who talked to the cops. Most of my customers are students. They don't like the cops. That's why they left."

"Don't worry about it," said Hans. "You're not causing us any problems. We're the ones getting you into trouble by coming to your café. From now on, we won't come by so often. Give the name Jules Montlouis for me," he added, lighting a cigarette.

"You have nothing to fear, Armando," insisted Jean de Dieu. "You don't know our real family names. Calm down, wipe your forehead and put on a smile back on your face. Everything will be fine."

"Another beautiful day to stay alive," said Hans with a wry smile.

The Brazilian and the African had heard these words so often, they didn't pay attention to them.

They waited for customers to come in again. There was a couple who wanted to toast their engagement. When Armando came back with coasters, his two friends had already left through the secret door.

Jenny Visits Jean de Dieu

Jean de Dieu had fed the stove with coal and had sat down in the little living room of his apartment on Rue Grégoire-de-Tours to read *The Cubist Painters: Aesthetic Meditations* by Guillaume Apollinaire. He had bought the book from a friendly bookseller on the Left Bank. Those cubists copied African masks and presented their copies as original. In reality, the "aesthetic meditations" were African. Outside, it was snowing, and an icy wind was whistling through the cracks in the window frames.

He was going to meet Hans the next day to plan how to evade the Gestapo surveillance and get into the prince's apartment. He was trying not to think about the risky day ahead of him. He had put away his book and dozed off for just a few minutes when he heard a soft knock on his door. He picked up his pistol, which was right at his feet, and went to the door without opening it. There was a second knock, even softer.

"Yes?"

"It's me," said Jenny quietly, so as not to alert his next-door neighbour.

Jean de Dieu put his weapon back under his chair and opened the door.

Jenny came in, wearing a black cotton coat with padded shoulders and a narrow waist, and a matching beret tilted to one side. "Thank you. It sure is cold tonight! Say, you have a nice place."

She looked around the little living room with the well-stocked bookcase, the two armchairs in stylized patterns, and the shag rug. The kitchen beside it was very narrow but seemed to have a place for everything. It was the first time she had come. Usually they saw each other at her place. He had wanted to avoid her being forced to give his address if she was ever questioned by the Nazis.

"Thank you. Give me your coat and go warm up by the stove. How did you get here? Are you sure you weren't followed?"

She rolled her eyes, annoyed. "You're not the only one who knows how to lose a tail. Besides, who would be suspicious of a little Chinese girl who works in a brothel? No one."

She untied the belt of her coat. Jean de Dieu observed that she was wearing a tight-fitting tweed skirt with a puffy-sleeved blouse and a sleeveless pullover, all in shades of forest green. She sat down, opened her handbag, and took out a cigarette, which she inserted in a cigarette holder. She waited, her eyes fixed on Jean de Dieu.

She was laying on the charm, and Jean de Dieu responded, pulling a box of matches from his pants pocket and striking one. He noted how the light of the flame brought out Jenny's cat-like eyes and her burgundy-painted lips. How could he resist her charms? But did he really want to? That was the second question he was asking himself as he put the matchbox back in his pants pocket. He offered her a glass of wine and she smiled with pleasure.

"I wouldn't want you to think I'm a tart you can get drunk with a glass of wine."

"Water, then?"

She replied that drinking water at this time of day was criminal.

"You're absolutely right."

They toasted her first visit to Jean de Dieu's place.

He noticed that she wasn't wearing nylons but had drawn lines down the backs of her calves to make it look as if she was. Seeing his eyes on her legs, she asked, "Do you mind if I put my feet close to the stove? I walked more than necessary because I wanted to make sure I wasn't followed."

He nodded yes. She took off her wooden-soled shoes.

She knew he was waiting for her report, and she didn't delay. "Major Baumeister is quite a rogue. He spends time with a certain Angèle who works at the Sphinx in the 14th arrondissement. You must know that house. Very posh. Before her, there was Ludmilla at the One-Two-Two in the 8th. But he abandoned her for Angèle. He likes the Aryan type, tall, blond, fair-skinned women with big behinds. Ludmilla was Polish and Angèle is Alsatian."

"And how did you learn all this?"

"I used to work at the One-Two-Two. I made a few friends I've stayed in contact with. I was the hostess of the 'Japanese room,' which wasn't far from the 'Egyptian room.' But I was turning four tricks a day. It was too much for me. I escaped to the Chat Botté. Lower pay but only three tricks a day, and tipping is mandatory."

"And this Angèle? Do you know her personally?"

"No. But in this line of work, you always know someone who knows someone. Why do you ask?"

It was only then that Jean de Dieu told her in detail what Baumeister had subjected him to. Jenny gazed at him with renewed intensity. She put her glass of wine down and said, "I've known men who are always ready to humiliate people for the pleasure of it."

She stood up and walked noiselessly to the window, which was covered with a dark curtain, and peeked outside. "I can imagine what he demands of Angèle for his pleasure. I always avoided the upper floors at the One-Two-Two. That sado-maso stuff isn't for me."

"Do you think Angèle would be prepared to do us a favour?"

She turned around and looked at him. She was silhouetted in the dim light. Jean de Dieu gazed appreciatively at her natural curves in the long, tight skirt.

"What do you mean exactly?"

"Compromising photos of them. We would hide Angèle's face."

"Maybe. I know someone who can introduce me to her. I'll sound her out."

"Be careful though."

"Stop saying that. I'm not important to you. I'm just an employee."

That comment made him smile. He stood up, went into the kitchen, and opened his little gas-powered Frigidaire refrigerator. He came back with a plate of hors d'oeuvres. He had managed to find eggs; a farmer came to his neighbourhood and sold them for an arm and a leg. He had also obtained a few sausages and some turnips, which he had garnished with mayonnaise and coarsely ground pepper.

Jenny was dumbfounded. "You're full of surprises. You did all this for me? That's so nice."

He sat down in the living room again. There was no dining room. They savoured the hors d'oeuvres with a second glass of wine. Jean de Dieu turned on the radio and searched for a station with soft music. He came across Tino Rossi singing "Marinella." He suggested they dance there in his little living room and she accepted happily. He confessed in a whisper that he'd fallen under her spell.

She made a point of looking into his eyes to make sure he wasn't toying with her. "A dangerous seducer. You waited until I was under your roof and made me melt like sugar in the sun."

They kissed and forgot there was a war on. They left a trail of clothing on the floor on their way to the bedroom. They disappeared under the comforter, resurfacing from time to time to catch their breath before going back to plumb the depths of their desire.

There were moments in the wee hours of the morning when whispers became keys that unlocked hearts and they shared secrets. Jean de Dieu told Jenny he remembered loving parents and a country with green hills. Cattle herders and farmers. He still understood a few words of the language he had spoken until the age of eight. Languages, more and more languages, which he deciphered with surprising ease. He also remembered a hut in flames with his parents inside after he had gone to fetch water from the river. With no family for kilometres around, he had been entrusted to White men in cassocks, with long beards, priests from Belgium, who took him to the Belgian Congo by train. One day, he told Jenny, when this damn war was over, he would return to that country of green hills. He would go and find those endless green mountains that he saw in his dreams almost every night in the heart of Paris. He would find Rwanda again.

As for Jenny, she had fled poverty. Her mother, who hadn't talked much, had toiled under the uncaring gaze of a drunkard husband who beat her and took opium. Jenny had left the house at fifteen, certain that she had found the love of her life. But once she was in Macao, there was disappointment. She had walked the streets to pay her boyfriend's drug debts. If it hadn't been for that Portuguese official, who was thirty years older than her and married, but crazy in love with her, Jenny would probably have died of exhaustion like her mother. In Lisbon, she had fled once again, far from that older man. She now dreamed of no longer running away, and of loving a man as Michelle Morgan loved Jean Gabin in *Le Quai des brumes*. She wanted someone to say to her, "You have beautiful eyes, you know." Yes, she was sentimental, but in this war, that was the best refuge.

They kissed, letting the dusky mantle of silence cover their confidences.

Hans and Jean de Dieu Against the Gestapo

Hans and Jean de Dieu devised a plan to get into the prince's apartment. They needed to get the money and the diamonds from the prince's safe, and make the evidence of his illicit business disappear. Jean de Dieu would keep the gems in a secure place pending the prince's return. The prince had also entrusted them with the mission of getting his companion Suzy and his son Rodolfo out of France.

The plan for getting into the apartment was finalized at Matty's house on Rue du Cap in Créteil. Jean de Dieu would take his semiautomatic pistol, equipped with a silencer. Hans would carry a Sten gun, a short submachine gun that was light and above all easy to hide. He had recruited Philippe, Matty's brother-in-law, in exchange for fifteen ration cards that he had gotten on the black market with money from Jean de Dieu. The cards included category T tickets, for workers who performed heavy labour. With those, you could get extra bread and meat. Philippe, who was barely making ends meet as a carpenter, had leapt at the opportunity. For a few extra tickets, he convinced his buddy Robert to join him. Philippe and Robert could have been boxers. They had broad shoulders, thick wrists, and rough hands. They swung hammers and moved furniture daily.

The two arrived in front of the building in La Muette in a sputtering gasogene-powered van in mid-afternoon. They were immediately spotted by two men in black coats and fedoras who were sitting in a front-wheel-drive car with the Citroën double chevron on the grille. The carpenters lifted a large piece of furniture out of their van. It looked like a dresser, but it had false drawer fronts. They went into the building through the back. One of the fedoras caught up with them in the lobby. He called out sharply, "Stop right there. Police. Where are you going? What floor?"

Philippe explained that they were making a delivery to the /third floor, Mme. Pinault's apartment.

The policeman had a scar across his chin to the left corner of his mouth. "Papers, and be quick," he ordered.

They took out their false documents with their actual photos on them. Jean de Dieu had gotten them good forgeries and the officer found nothing amiss. He checked the list of tenants to see if there was in fact a woman named Pinault. He quickly found what he was looking for. He scratched his chin, looked at the dresser, and decided to let them carry it upstairs without accompanying them. The men took back their documents and started climbing the stairs. The dresser was heavy, but it was important that they not show how difficult it was to carry. The Gestapo man turned and went to report to his colleague at the wheel of the Citroën. The two officers were fed up with watching the place. They would rather be torturing dark-skinned foreigners and murdering Communists. Instead they were surveilling the Paris residence of an African prince who was in Portugal. Baumeister, whom they called "Le Boche," had a screw loose.

The fedora waiting in the Citroën was blackmailing an aristocrat whose twenty-year-old son had been caught putting up anti-Nazi posters. He was in a hurry to go off duty. He planned to take his dough and blow it in a clandestine gambling den that offered "all the champagne you can drink and a couple of broads to take care of you all night long," as he had told his partner.

The partner walked back to the car muttering. He didn't look happy. The officer in the car immediately understood that they were just dealing with a couple of workers carrying a dresser. He returned to his daydreams of drink and debauchery, drumming his dirty fingernails on the steering wheel.

The two carpenters stopped on the second floor. Robert quietly went back down alone to check that the coast was clear. He signaled to Philippe, who opened the back panel of the dresser. Without a word, Jean de Dieu climbed painfully out of the dresser, his forehead beaded with sweat. When he was back on his feet, he promised himself never again to get into a piece of furniture too short for his legs. Hoping not to run into another tenant, he quickly went up to the top floor, unlocked the door of the prince's apartment, and closed it behind him without turning the key.

Philippe and Robert picked up the dresser again, carrying it without difficulty. They pushed open the door to Prince Antonio's apartment and put it down in the living room. They wiped it down from top to bottom to erase any trace of their hands even though they were wearing work gloves. Then they took their time going back downstairs and getting into the van. They started the vehicle and drove away under the indifferent gaze of the two officers in the Citroën. They stopped just far enough away to no longer be seen by the Gestapo officers.

Hans was keeping a lookout in a café across from where they parked the van. He paid his bill and joined his comrades in the cab, his submachine gun under his coat. The compact weapon could pepper the Citroën with bullets if it should take chase. The three men remained silent, waiting impatiently for Jean de Dieu's return. Philippe was on his second cigarette. They couldn't keep the van parked in that affluent neighbourhood very long. Robert was biting his nails, and Hans, expressionless, was counting the minutes in his head.

Meanwhile, Jean de Dieu had grabbed a black briefcase and was filling it with banknotes from the safe in the prince's closet. The prince had left about 50,000 francs in it before leaving for Lisbon. The African heard the apartment door creak. He closed the briefcase and took his semi-automatic Ruby out of his ankle holster. He crept quietly back to the living room. No one. Philippe and Robert, in their haste, had forgotten to close the door. He shut it, locked it, and put away his weapon. Briefcase in hand, he went over to the window. He opened the curtain rod on the right and took out some precious stones, a dozen diamonds. He placed them in the false bottom of the briefcase.

He was getting ready to leave when there was a knock on the door. He grabbed his pistol again, tempted to shoot through the door. But what if it was the carpenters, impatient? He put the briefcase down behind the door and kept the weapon behind his back. "Who is it?"

"It's me, Simon, your neighbour."

Simon Giraudoux, alias Pastis. The informer.

Jean de Dieu opened the door, keeping the pistol concealed in the hollow of his back. "Simon, is everything all right? Did you want to talk to Prince Antonio?"

The bootlegger took a step back, a forced smile on his lips. "Yes, to welcome him back. I've noticed he's been absent these last weeks. Is he here?"

"Yes, come in. He'd like to say hello to you."

Simon hesitated for a moment, realizing that he had left his weapon in a drawer in his apartment. Always so impulsive. He tried to convince himself that there was no risk with this young man who was always smiling and affable. He was only a translator.

Once inside, he felt the barrel of a pistol on his temple. "I…"

"Shut up."

Jean de Dieu checked that he wasn't carrying a weapon and said, "You're the one who ratted on the prince to the cops, right?"

"No! Not at all. I'm a friend. I never would have done that! I don't understand why there's a problem."

Jean de Dieu had figured out that Simon was the informer because the newspapers had reported the arrest of a major bootlegger in the 16th arrondissement. What was he doing home again? Why had the police let him go? "You're a police informer. Admit it. I saw the police report that accused the prince. I saw it! Your name is in it. In black and white. Simon Giraudoux, alias Pastis."

He wanted to see if Giraudoux would fall into the trap. He stuck the barrel of the gun with the silencer in the man's mouth. "Answer me. But one more lie and I'll decorate the wall with your brains."

His icy stare terrified Pastis. The man wasn't bluffing. His dark gaze was threatening. Giraudoux didn't realize that the African had known his alias for a long time.

Jean de Dieu withdrew the gun barrel from Pastis's mouth to allow him to answer.

"They made me do it. They hung me upside down. I was bleeding all over. They were going to keep torturing me. Listen, how much will it cost to keep you quiet? Don't say anything to the prince. I'll give you double what he pays you. I'll triple what you earn. You'll have all the money you need!"

"Is the cash in your apartment?"

"Yes," said the informer, relieved.

Jean de Dieu had decided to kill Giraudoux in his own apartment. The two men walked a few metres down the corridor and entered the apartment. Under Jean de Dieu's watchful gaze, Giraudoux lowered his arms and opened the drawer of his desk. Facing Jean de Dieu, he put his hand into the drawer to grab hold of his Smith & Wesson revolver. Alerted, Jean de Dieu put a bullet in Pastis's right eye, and the informer collapsed to the floor. Dead instantly.

Jean de Dieu saw the revolver, which had fallen not far from Pastis's bloody eye. It was a six-round .38, heavy and threatening. The barrel was long, about 12 centimetres. It occurred to him that it was difficult to take out such a revolver quickly. There was no money in the drawer. Too bad, he would have taken it without hesitation.

Jean de Dieu retrieved his briefcase from the prince's apartment before quickly heading down the stairs. There was a retired couple waiting for the elevator on the second floor, but he avoided them and continued his descent, then turned to the left to go out the back door of the building.

A policeman with a luxuriant moustache and a kepi on his head was approaching the van. Philippe, at the wheel of the vehicle, saw him in the rear-view mirror. Hans, inside the van with him and Robert, took the submachine gun from inside his coat.

"Put that away, I'll take care of this," said Philippe.

The officer addressed Philippe. What was he doing here? It was forbidden to park so close to a bus stop. Philippe replied that he was having some minor mechanical problems. "You know these gas vehicles, they're very touchy." The motor had overheated, and he had to give it time to cool down.

The officer would have none of it. "Get moving," he ordered, pointing an accusing finger.

Philippe looked at Robert and Hans. "We'll have to leave."

Hans was about to get out to go to the prince's apartment. If his friend was having problems, he wanted to help him. Someone knocked on the passenger-side door. It was Jean de Dieu, briefcase in hand. "Can you make a little room for me?"

"Of course," Hans answered, with a broad smile. "Hurry up and get in."

Robert laughed, glad to get out of there. He was sitting very close to Philippe, who was having trouble shifting gears. The van headed towards Créteil with the four men happy to get away safe and sound.

Prince Antonio Prepares to Return

The prince had made the rounds of his Lisbon connections, selling his country's coffee. He'd visited an administrator at Hotel Avenida, not far from the Bairro Alto and Chiado neighbourhoods. The man appreciated Angolan products and he had bought a large quantity of coffee. Then the prince had hired a taxi and gone to Estoril in the suburbs of Lisbon, eighteen kilometres west of the capital. There he had met with the business manager of Hotel Palácio, who had purchased many bags stamped "Coffee Product of Angola." The prince had taken the opportunity to sell to the casinos on the Costa do Sol before returning to the capital. He had one more customer left to see at the Tavares restaurant in Chiado. There, in a few days, he would be able to unload his last remaining bags of coffee. He had stored them in a warehouse in the port of Lisbon by agreement with a customs agent who was on his payroll. A delivery man would take care of distributing the merchandise to the customers once the prince gave him the green light.

Since his return, he had been finding the atmosphere in his city rather bleak. The faces of the Lisbon residents were morose, and the refugees, worried and suspicious, walked the streets like ghosts with chains on their feet. Although the bourgeoisie were still partying and going out to the fancy hotels, it felt as if they were laughing to keep from crying. The power was in the hands of politicians who spoke of the *Estado Novo*. Although Prince Antonio avoided getting involved in Portuguese politics, he observed that Lisbonites in the "New State" kept as quiet as mice when they saw a uniform.

The prince had purchased some cigars at Tabacaria Mónaco on Plaça do Rossio. He was in a restaurant on Rua da Prata smoking one, and sipping an iced port with a slice of lemon while looking at the menu. He was preoccupied by another question. He had a distinct feeling that he was being followed and spied on whenever he left home. The taxi driver who had driven him to Estoril had even mentioned that a vehicle had been behind them all the way from Lisbon. The prince had told him not to worry about it. He knew that spies in the pay of the Nazis were probably on his tail. Even the NKVD, the Soviet spy agency, must be after him. He had sold diamonds to Russians, who would surely be happy to turn him into an agent working for them. Nevertheless, he knew that as long as he didn't make any missteps, it would be difficult to blackmail him into becoming a spy. He was walking a tightrope, but that was what was required by the times.

A bon vivant, Prince Antonio would have preferred to enjoy luxuries and beautiful women. However, his taste for the pleasures of life did not make him a man without principles. He read the newspapers and kept up on the situation in the world. As Jean de Dieu had said to him in Swahili, "*Ada ya mja hunena, Muungwana ni kitendo.*" A man talks, but a gentleman acts. Neither the Nazis nor the Communists would prevent him from returning one day to reign in his kingdom in Angola.

After his evening meal, the prince paid his bill, adding a nice tip. He knew that to maintain a good reputation, you had to spoil people who worked for you. That way you increased the chances that one of them would warn you of potential danger.

Once back on the street, the prince decided to go to his next destination on foot. A cold wind from the Atlantic was sweeping through the city. He instinctively turned up the collar of his wool coat. He could have taken one of the trams that threaded their way through the streets. Their electrical crackling and their headlights in the dusk made them seem like extraterrestrial creatures. But he wasn't going far, just to Rua dos Douradores, and he wanted to digest his dinner while walking. He had eaten early so that he would have time for a discussion with an influential man, perhaps his most important acquaintance in Lisbon. The two men did each other favours and got along almost like friends. Of course, in these difficult and uncertain times, Prince Antonio did not dare call Senhor Miranda a friend.

After serving with the military in Angola, Miranda had become a business lawyer. He had been the Portuguese Minister of Justice for a year. Senhor Santiago Afonso Rodrigo Miranda had a large portrait of the country's strongman, Antonio de Oliveira Salazar, in his office.

The prince walked through the entrance, where a guard was dozing. He knocked softly on a door with the lawyer's initials on it. Miranda's secretary, a woman in her fifties, gave him a perfunctory smile. He visited her boss often enough for her not to make him wait. She immediately ushered him into the lawyer's office. Miranda, pen in hand, motioned the prince to a luxurious armchair. He stopped writing, smiled broadly, and came and shook his visitor's hand. "Welcome home, Prince Antonio. Lisbon has become your city, hasn't it?" Without waiting for the prince's answer, he turned his head and said, "Rosalina, you may leave. And lock the door please!"

"Yes, Senhor."

When they were alone, with the door double-locked, the two men quickly got down to the matter at hand. Neither one of them liked to beat around the bush.

"Go ahead, my friend."

"I want to go back to Paris," began the prince. "I left some stones there. They're worth a fortune. But the Nazis will pick me up at the train station to question me, and I don't have to tell you their methods. They know about my business."

The lawyer knew what the prince did for a living. And he found the fees the prince paid for his services very satisfactory. "You know that, here, you have nothing to fear. Why don't you stay in Lisbon? You can conduct your business here. There are enough rich clients to make you happy. And if anything at all goes wrong, I'll defend you."

"That's what I intend to do. But I have to recover my stones."

The lawyer crossed his legs and asked, "How will you get the stones out without getting nabbed by the Gestapo?"

"I left a translator and a driver in Paris. They'll help me."

The lawyer scratched his chin, puzzled. He raised his bushy eyebrows and squinted questioningly. "A translator and a driver?"

"I know it may seem hard to believe, but they're vital to my business. Loyal and capable."

"They must be exceptional employees."

"Yes, they're special."

The lawyer concluded that it was best not to ask for further details. That way, when the day came that he had to defend Prince Antonio, he wouldn't have any information about his business or his employees. "Do you have something to propose to me?"

"Yes. I am offering to remove a thorn from your government's side."

The prince had heard about the arrest of Leandro Barros, the head of a fascist paramilitary organization. He proposed that he take Barros to Paris and unite him with his Nazi comrades.

Barros had been calling for a Berlin-Lisbon axis in all his speeches. Infuriated, Salazar had thrown him into prison. His organization, the Brigada Suprema, had been outlawed. Since Portugal's government claimed to be neutral, Salazar had to maintain that position, at least in appearance.

Senhor Miranda shot the prince an admiring glance. What he liked about this African was his ability to land on his feet. Like a cat. "Rumour has it," the lawyer said, "that he's going to be sent to Tarrafal, on Cape Verde. If Salazar does that, it could cause an uprising. Barros is very popular with young people, and outlawing his organization has already made them unhappy."

Both men knew what "Tarrafal" meant. A concentration camp for adversaries of the regime. It was certain death. The place had no running water. Even the guards were dying of disease.

"I can take Barros to his German friends in Paris. He idolizes Hitler and Mussolini. And your government would be rid of him. Getting him out could prevent serious consequences."

"But we can't just give the Nazis a gift. That would jeopardize our position with the British and their allies. We would have to get something in return," replied the lawyer.

"I can bring back Father Eusébio da Silva, who was arrested by the Germans when he arrived in Paris."

The lawyer smiled in admiration. "You've really thought of everything."

Father Eusébio da Silva was a well-known Portuguese priest who taught religious studies at the Sorbonne, and who had been arrested by the Nazis for speaking out against the persecution of the Jews. He had also sent a copy of the Ten Commandments to the military governor of Paris.

"I was in a nearby café when the Nazis arrested him," said the prince. "He was brandishing an image of Jesus on the cross in front of the Institut d'Étude des Questions Juives [Institute for the study of Jewish questions] on Rue La Boétie. The Gestapo hauled him away brutally."

"Eusébio da Silva," repeated Miranda. "The Vatican would be very grateful to us. The pope would bless Salazar. Although the Church said nothing after his arrest, the Catholic family is always concerned about its lost sheep."

He went to the little bar behind his large desk and took out two glasses and a bottle of forty-year-old port. After filling the glasses, he made a toast: "Long live our enlightened leader!"

The prince smiled and toasted with the lawyer. "Long live Salazar!" He drank, thanking his lucky stars that he had connections with well-placed people.

"Give me a little time," said the lawyer. "I'll have to talk to a few bigwigs in the government. But I think your proposal will please my leaders. Just one thing..."

"What's that?" asked the prince, lowering his glass, concerned.

"I can't tell them it's your idea. A proposal like that coming from a Black man, especially one from Angola, our colony, it wouldn't be taken seriously. They'd be blinded by your ancestry and refuse the whole thing. I'll have to steal the idea from you."

The prince felt a pang. It was always the same. His every victory was snatched from him. He received no recognition for anything he did here. That was why he wanted to go back to Angola one day and bring independence to his country. As soon as he arrived in the White world, he had been assigned his rank and his place. Since then, he had been living on the margins. Because he couldn't count on the good faith of others, he had created his own code of conduct, his principles, and his limits. "No problem, you can have my idea," he replied. "No hard feelings, my dear Santiago."

They drank just one glass each since it was getting late. The streets of Lisbon at night in those times of political uncertainty could be full of bandits and cutthroats. The former minister's car was at the garage. They took a taxi together. They arrived at Prince Antonio's destination first. When he tried to pay his fare, Senhor Miranda shook his head. "No, I'll take care of it. Our conversation in the office was well worth it."

The prince closed the car door and walked away with a smile on his lips. The farther away he got, the more he felt he had come out the winner in the transaction. He would probably see Paris again, and Jean de Dieu and Hans. Once again he would get the better of the Nazis, tricking them like silly soldiers in an operetta.

Headaches for the Major

Major Baumeister had just taken an aspirin to ward off the migraine he felt coming. In a fit of rage, he had thrown his empty glass against the wall of his office. Magda was silently sweeping up the shards in a corner of the room. He could hear the typewriters of the other secretaries on the floor, and that made his headache worse. He reread the report that had caused his anger.

> *Murder of Simon Giraudoux, alias Pastis, shot in the right eye with a 7.65 calibre bullet. The death occurred about three days ago according to the medical examiner.*

This demoralized him. He would no longer be able to confront Prince Antonio with the informer. That was always an excellent interrogation technique. In the course of his denials, the suspect usually ended up giving himself away. Earlier in the day, after getting the bad news, he had sent Lieutenant Betz to the Angolan's apartment. An hour later, the young officer had confirmed that visitors had gotten in there without the Gestapo men's knowledge. Betz had mentioned a dresser in the living room that hadn't been there during their first visit. The officers who had been surveilling the place admitted that they had seen two big guys carry a dresser up there three days before. Their description was of two strapping Frenchmen, Whites. The bad news didn't stop there. Baumeister's men had discovered a safe concealed in the back of a huge closet in the prince's apartment. It had been emptied of its contents. The major had read a rebuke in his lieutenant's eyes. He should have had the place searched earlier. He massaged his temples. But he wouldn't have been able to pocket the diamonds if there had been an official search. His general would have claimed the precious gems. The loot would have ended up in somebody else's pocket.

And how was he going to explain this failure? His superior, General Erich von Bose, had had him in the hot seat ever since a Black had murdered two policemen from Rue Lauriston. Of course, it wasn't Germans who'd been killed, but it made relations difficult with the French Gestapo. In addition, the investigation into the whereabouts of that damn translator was stalled. Yes, a young man who looked like him had been seen on the Left Bank. But there were so many slender, elegant Blacks in Paris! The composite sketch could be of an African, a Caribbean man, or an American.

Baumeister absent-mindedly took his monocle out of the pocket of his uniform, rubbed the lens, and placed it in his right eye. His thoughts took him back to Vienna, where he used to torture Communists in the basement of Hotel Metropole, near the Danube Canal. What he was planning for that African who called himself João de Deus Kassoma was the application of electricity to his genitals. He recalled the man standing stark naked in front of him. He had thought of it then, but had concluded that he was insignificant. He had seen only a scrawny intellectual who read books on ethnology in the bathtub, listening to Charles Trenet. An unimportant pencil pusher.

However, since that memorable encounter, the Nazi had realized that the translator played a bigger role in Prince Antonio's diamond smuggling. Who else could have gotten back into the prince's apartment when it was under surveillance? He must have entered the building inside that damn dresser. And he'd bet on the head of his wife, who was waiting patiently for him in Berlin, that the translator was roaming around Paris armed with a semi-automatic, the weapon that had killed his informer.

The man had played him for a fool. There were, after all, a few Blacks to whom nature, with no apparent logic, had been generous. He'd been at the Olympic Stadium in Berlin in 1936 when Jesse Owens, that chimpanzee with primitive energy, had won four medals. Was it possible that the translator had the gift of cunning just as the champion had the gift of speed? The Nazi was beginning to think so.

He shouted for Betz. The strategy of the investigation would have to be reviewed. He was to speak with General Erich von Bose in a few hours. He couldn't face his superior without something positive to tell him.

The young officer came in and gave the Hitler salute, clicking his heels as was his habit. He could do it ten times a day. The major suspected Betz of thinking too highly of himself. His uniform always impeccable, not a hair on his head out of place, perfectly polished boots, and manicured fingernails. Baumeister found that last detail very intriguing. He had checked with a colleague whether Betz had a lady friend in Paris or if he visited brothels. Neither was the case, and suspicions of homosexuality had taken root in his mind. However, destroying the career of the son of a German industrialist on a question of morality was risky. Such a ploy could backfire. The children of the rich were untouchable, even under the Nazi regime.

"So, Lieutenant, how's the hunt for the translator going?"

"We've infiltrated the intellectual crowd on the Left Bank, sounded out philosophers who support our cause, and questioned the academic staff at the Institut d'Ethnologie, without much success. He hasn't been going to classes, and he gave them the address in La Muette as his residence."

The major stood up and went to the window. The monocle fell from his right eye. He put it back in with an almost comical grimace. Betz kept his nose in his papers.

"But Prince Antonio has a driver, doesn't he?" asked Baumeister.

"Yes, a guy named Jules Montlouis, from Martinique. But there's something strange."

"What's that?"

"Jules Montlouis speaks German. A waiter at the jazz club La Cigale heard him chitchatting with a German-speaking Black musician named Matty."

"A Martinican who speaks fluent German?" asked Baumeister.

The young officer nodded.

Betz's words had hit home. Baumeister said, "I want a tail on Matty." He'd been about to say "the saxophonist," but stopped himself. He didn't want to reveal that he knew who the man was. His ex, Ludmilla, was a fan of the musician. He had tolerated that in her because she was good in bed.

"If the driver is friends with Matty, we'll be able to pick him up," said Baumeister, smiling malevolently. The aspirin was relieving his headache. "We have a trio of polyglots, Lukas. A prince who speaks Portuguese, a translator who speaks French, and a driver who speaks German. There's something fishy about all this. Do you have a description of Montlouis?"

"Yes, Major. We're dealing with a group of subhuman diamond smugglers who deserve the firing squad."

Baumeister swore. "I didn't ask you what those Blacks deserved. I want to know if the Caribbean man is light brown, dark brown, or black as night. Do you have a description?"

The lieutenant quickly searched through the papers on his lap. "Brown complexion, possibly mulatto."

"Contact the Rhineland documentation centre. I want a list of those bastards who've entered France. Those mulattos avoided sterilization, and some of them speak French because their fathers were Senegalese soldiers sent to the Rhineland."

The young man took note of his orders without saying a word. He knew that if he kept quiet his superior's anger might dissipate. He had been warned before his transfer to Paris. The man was hot-tempered and homophobic. But this was a posting in the world capital of fashion. It was the city of Coco Chanel. Who could refuse? The Louvre, the Eiffel Tower, the Arc de Triomphe. If things went sour with his boss, he could always call his father, who would get him another posting, maybe in Norway. He liked winter sports, the fjords, and saunas.

"What information do you have from our agents in Lisbon?" Baumeister asked. "Will the prince be returning soon?"

Lukas answered confidently. "According to the information available to us, he's almost finished selling his father's coffee to the hotels in the city. He should be back soon. Oh yes, we also know that he recently visited a lawyer close to the Portuguese government."

"Is he a spy for Salazar?"

The question seemed more for himself than for his subordinate. But Lukas took it upon himself to answer. "It's hard to say. Our spies have never had any dealings with him. And he's not on any lists of the Portuguese secret police."

This irritated the major even more. "I'm familiar with the Polícia de Vigilância e de Defesa do Estado. I knew them when you were still in short pants and perhaps had ribbons in your hair! Sorry, but I don't know what it's like to be born with a silver spoon in your mouth." The major stood up and rubbed his temples again. The migraine was threatening to come back. "According to his file, Prince Antonio is a bit of a skirt chaser. Is there any woman in particular? One he likes more than the others?"

"His bank account in Paris doesn't show any cheques made out to a specific mistress. But…" Lieutenant Betz hesitated because he didn't want to be snapped at again.

"But what?"

"Before he left, he was making regular payments to a woman who owns a hairdressing salon on Rue de Rennes."

"Ah. And you didn't think to mention it to me?"

"I believed it was for illegal coal sales."

"You're not paid to make deductions, Lieutenant Betz."

The young man blushed but remained silent, his eyes fixed on the file.

"So we do have something," declared Baumeister slyly, seeing his lieutenant's embarrassment. "What is it? Do your bourgeois principles prevent you from going after lovebirds?"

"No, Major. The salon owner is twice his age."

"Maybe he was seeing her daughter. In any case, we need to get to the bottom of this. I want that hairdresser in my office as soon as possible."

"Yes, Sir."

"Dismissed. I have to write a report for General von Bose on the number of deaths under torture. I've tried to tell him you can't make an omelette without breaking eggs, but he's demanding more subjects who've confessed their crimes and are still alive. If it were up to him, we'd have to bring the resistance fighters back to life and interrogate them again."

Lieutenant Betz acted as if he hadn't heard his superior's words and closed the door. In Baumeister's eyes, Betz had never known real work and was rising through the ranks without shedding any blood. He was a desk Nazi. And a daddy's boy too. He didn't consider him reliable. What had he done to deserve a right-hand man who cared so much about his appearance and refused to get his hands dirty? He raised his gaze to the heavens, hoping for an answer. There was only silence.

To put himself in a better mood, he thought about his current mistress, Angèle. He was seeing her tonight. They were going to a very popular play at the Théâtre des Champs-Élysées, and then ending the night in his four-poster bed, where Angèle was given erotic punishments. The major already felt better. Now he could finally concentrate on counting up the dead at the hands of the Gestapo.

Suzy Lazowski and Her Little Rodolfo

For two days, Jean de Dieu had been observing Suzy Lazowski's comings and goings. He was trying to find a way to approach her without setting off alarm bells. Suzy had met him only once, by chance, in the métro, in the company of the prince, who had made the introductions without saying more. Had it not been for his employer's letter, he would never have known where her apartment was. The prince had always been discreet about her in order to shield her from his covert activities.

Jean de Dieu realized she was keeping a low profile. But that wouldn't necessarily protect her, because the police could intern her at any time under the Act Relating to Aliens of Jewish Race, which had been enacted in 1940. And she continued working as a hairdresser in a salon on Rue de Rennes.

Her boss, Pierrette, a matronly woman in her fifties, had asked her cousin, who was a police commissioner, to see that her employee was at the bottom of any internment list. The prince was aware of this. He had been thinking of a way to get her out of France when the problems arose with Baumeister.

Pierrette was fond of Suzy. She was a good worker, and Pierrette had also taken a liking to her little boy, Rodolfo, who was barely two years old. The chubby-cheeked toddler with a milk chocolate complexion would cling to her neck as soon as Suzy passed him to her. Suzy brought the child with her to work. Pierrette had a nursery upstairs and took care of her employees' children with the help of a niece. She felt like a grandmother to Rodolfo.

Hans had suggested going to Suzy's home, in the 19th arrondissement, and using the pretext of selling something in order to talk to her. It was a good idea, but Jean de Dieu felt that the young woman would be on her guard and would not open the door to anyone she didn't know. His observation of her had revealed her to be a woman who was wary, who kept her eyes lowered and preferred crowded trains so as not to be noticed by the German soldiers. However, deportation seemed inevitable.

On the third day, Jean de Dieu decided he would go to her place of work and talk to the owner. He wanted Pierrette's help to convince Suzy to flee with him. The woman would understand how important it was for her employee to get out of Paris. Jean de Dieu figured that if Pierrette was employing a Jewish woman, she must not share the views of the Nazis and their collaborators.

He waited a few minutes in the café Les Rois Mages near the hairdressing salon. He was wearing a dark blue coat with padded shoulders, and his hat, a black fedora with a white ribbon, went well with his black suit and his necktie with a blue fleur-de-lys pattern. He finished the last of his croissant and drained his coffee, which was actually just chicory. The other patrons of the café seemed too busy chatting to pay attention to him. But he knew that this was not the case. There was always someone on the lookout for the slightest piece of information that could interest German intelligence. People became informants because they were starving or being coerced, or simply because they were opportunists.

Jean de Dieu folded his newspaper, *Le Petit Parisien*, under his arm, pulled the brim of his hat down, and went outside. He was about to cross the street to Chez Pierrette when a front-wheel-drive Citroën screeched to a stop in front of the building. He thought it best to make a sharp turn, but he didn't go far. He joined the line waiting outside the neighbourhood bakery. Such lines were becoming common in the city because of shortages. The car doors slammed and Jean de Dieu recognized the Nazi officer who had barged into Prince Antonio's bathroom, Lieutenant Betz. He was clean-shaven, with fine features, and was wearing an impeccable uniform. Jean de Dieu opened his newspaper and watched him surreptitiously. Betz went into the hairdressing salon accompanied by two other soldiers.

Jean de Dieu was filled with remorse. He should have contacted her earlier. Why had he waited two days to talk to her? The prince would never see Suzy and his son again. He felt terrible about it. But would she have believed him if he had approached her in the street? Two more ladies joined the line. Jean de Dieu peeked over his newspaper and saw that the Gestapo was leaving with a fat lady in her fifties. They were taking Pierrette in. Maybe the major had made a strategic error. Suzy and the boy were not lost!

The car drove off quickly, watched by the passersby. Four women, one of them Suzy, came out on the doorstep of the salon, upset at the arrest of their boss. Then they went back inside to take care of the customers.

Jean de Dieu felt a hand on his shoulder and turned brusquely.

"Monsieur, the line is moving forward." The woman, in her forties, backed away a bit after his abrupt movement.

"Oh. I can't wait anymore. You can have my place."

He slipped the newspaper inside his coat and crossed the street to the hairdressing salon. There was a commotion inside and Jean de Dieu took advantage of it to speak to Suzy, who had just ushered a customer to her chair. "Mademoiselle?"

She turned, taken aback.

"Prince Antonio is outside and wants to talk to you."

The other hairdressers stopped what they were doing, and a lady in her thirties came over.

"May I help you?"

He turned a deaf ear to her and immediately went back out, hoping Suzy would follow him. All he heard was the murmuring of the women, who were wondering what that Black man was doing here. He mustn't give them enough time to fix his face in their memory. He suspected that the Gestapo was circulating a composite sketch of him.

"Monsieur?" It was Suzy approaching on the sidewalk, puzzled. "Where is he? Has he come back?"

Jean de Dieu wanted to take her to a quiet place to explain the situation she was in but he sensed that Suzy wasn't going to budge from that sidewalk. The passersby were walking quickly, and bicycle taxis and a few city buses were moving along Rue de Rennes.

"He's not here. He's still in Lisbon."

She seemed to lose her composure when she heard that. She paled and shook her head in disbelief.

Just when she was going to turn and leave, he gripped her forearm and pulled her close so he could speak softly. "I'm Jean de Dieu, the prince's translator. We met once. Do you recall?"

She frowned, trying to place him.

"The men who picked Pierrette up will come back for you. You're no longer safe in the hairdressing salon. I'll help you. I'll be waiting in the café up the street. Find a way to join me there."

"I don't remember you. Do you know why they took Pierrette away?"

There was the sound of a siren in the distance and Jean de Dieu glanced around to see if it was coming for them. Hearing the sound receding, he played his last card. "No. But I suspect they'll make her talk. And your name will come out. Suzy, you have to believe me. It was Prince Antonio who asked me to help you."

Her lips were trembling. She seemed to want to take her chances with him. But she gave him a desperate look. "I can't. My son is upstairs. I can't leave without him," she exclaimed.

He persisted. "Go get him. Tell the other hairdressers that I'm his father and that I'm going to take you to the Jardin du Luxembourg. Come join me in that café," he said pointing to Les Rois Mages.

Suzy didn't answer. She walked away. Then she quickly came back. "What's Prince Antonio's name?" she asked.

"Antonio Jose Henrique Dos Santos Mbwafu of the Kingdom of Kongo."

The fact that he knew her prince's full name and that he had said it without the least hesitation reassured her. "I'll be right there."

Relieved, Jean de Dieu went to a phone booth nearby and called Armando's café. He asked if they gave student discounts for their house sandwich. Armando said yes and the call ended. His question was a coded message telling Hans to come and get them in the car.

Hans left Armando and set off in his boss's car to pick up Jean de Dieu, Suzy, and Rodolfo. The Renault was unrecognizable, black now, with twelve-hole rims, chromeless headlights, and on the roof, three gas cylinders. Of course, all that had cost a lot. The nest egg in the prince's safe had paid the bill.

He took Rue de Vaugirard and then went around the Jardin du Luxembourg. That was the fastest route. He drove carefully, not wanting to hit any of the bicycle taxis that were taking up more and more space in the streets.

In the meantime, Suzy arrived at the café with Rodolfo, who was bundled up against the Parisian cold. Jean de Dieu stepped onto the sidewalk and took her hand as if they were a couple. They sat down in a quiet corner of the café. They would have to wait patiently for Hans. A mixed couple with a young child would not go unnoticed in the métro. Hans's car was the obvious choice. The child stared intently at the African. His little hat was slipping off, and his mother put it back on his head over his brown curls.

The barman brought Jean de Dieu and Suzy each a black coffee. A few customers were looking at them because of the child. It was midday and there weren't many people there. Jean de Dieu didn't want the little boy to make a scene in this unfamiliar environment. He ordered a glass of warm milk for him and spoke to his mother in a calm voice. "We're waiting for a car. It won't be long. It's the prince's driver."

"Hans?"

"Yes. You know him?"

"No, but the prince mentioned his name a few times."

Jean de Dieu was a bit disappointed that his employer hadn't mentioned his name.

Suzy, anxious, had turned her back to the café window as if she didn't want to know what was coming. Jean de Dieu noticed that she was trembling and was not able to give the milk to her son. He took her hand again, rubbed it because it was icy, and with a tender smile said in a low voice, "Let's hold the glass together. People who are watching us will look away. Lovers are always harmless."

Suzy smiled slightly in agreement and they gave the milk to the child. The little boy, focusing on the treat, forgot to look at that man in the big hat who was next to his mother.

"What's his name?" asked Jean de Dieu.

"Rodolfo. His full name is Rodolfo Prince Henri Junior Dos Santos Mbawfu."

"The heir," he said, smiling.

Hans got there in ten minutes. He knew they were waiting in the café and slowed down in front of it. When Jean de Dieu saw him, he motioned to Suzy to pass the child to him. She hesitated a few seconds. The African had his arms open. "Don't worry. He won't cry."

Jean de Dieu had a natural gentleness about him that calmed the child. Rodolfo let himself be carried, a bit anxious but with no tears. His mother gave him a big smile and stroked his cheek, murmuring to him in baby talk.

They walked out like that, Suzy diverting the child with a rattle she had taken out of her bag. His head on Jean de Dieu's shoulder, the child burped, and Suzy wiped his mouth.

Hans spotted them in his rear-view mirror and stopped the car a few metres away. They got in quickly and he headed towards the home of Armando and his wife, Nadège. Jean de Dieu handed the child back to his mother. For several minutes they rode in silence with the child on Suzy's lap.

Jean de Dieu spoke to her in a reassuring tone of voice. They weren't going far, just behind Le Croissant Doré, near the Sorbonne. Nadège, a Parisian married to a Brazilian, lived in a two-bedroom apartment. The couple had no children.

When would she be able to talk to Antonio? Suzy asked.

They would have to wait a few days, he answered, without saying more. The important thing was to try not to worry. She was in good hands with him and Hans. Nothing bad could happen to her now.

Once there, they got out quickly. Jean de Dieu ordered Hans to drive around the block and come back for him. He wasn't going to hang around. Hans smiled at the baby and said "See you soon" to Suzy, who answered with a smile.

On the second floor of an old building, Nadège, a petite brunette in her late thirties, quickly opened the door after two knocks, and Jean de Dieu stepped back to let the mother and child enter.

Nadège immediately put Suzy at ease. She spoke in a soft voice and showed her her room and the toiletries she would need. Suzy suddenly realized she had left her papers and those of her son at her place. Jean de Dieu told her then what he hadn't dared tell her in the car for fear of increasing her anxiety. She would never go back there.

"Give me the keys to your apartment and make a list of what I should get for you. I'll go there with Hans."

He gave her a piece of paper and a pen. The woman wrote mechanically. There were her original papers, the baby's birth certificate, a few bank notes hidden in her pillow for emergencies, and her reading glasses. She added a few other things, including a photo of her parents, who had died in a concentration camp. But Jean de Dieu, speaking softly, said he certainly would not be able to get all that.

Resigning herself, she handed him the paper, sat down on the bed she would be sleeping in, and stroked her son's hair. The milk had made the child fall asleep. Nadège brought her a Brazilian hot chocolate and reassured her again that she and the child had nothing to fear in this place.

Jean de Dieu quickly left the building and got into the car. Hans headed towards La Villette. They had to get there before the major's men. They knew they were taking a risk. But they needed to get rid of Suzy's photos in order to keep the Germans off their trail long enough for Suzy and her son to join Prince Antonio.

A Productive Conversation Between Jenny and Angèle

Jenny wasn't working that evening. She was waiting for Angèle, the major's mistress, in a fashionable restaurant on Rue du Cherche-Midi. She had introduced herself to Angèle the day before as a former employee of the Sphinx, the establishment where Angèle offered her services when she wasn't with the major. Angèle was curious as to why this Chinese woman, a prostitute like herself, wanted to meet her in a swanky Parisian restaurant. She guessed that her colleague must be recruiting for a sex party. She showed up at the appointed time.

Jenny treated Angèle to a generous dinner and plied her with first-rate German champagne. While the restaurant couldn't compare to Maxim's, it was growing in popularity. A dinner there could cost as much as 500 francs, while a good spread in a neighbourhood bistro would go for 18 francs. Jenny, dressed to the nines, presented herself as a sympathetic co-worker who shared the trials and tribulations of the trade. The patrons of the restaurant included many Germans, accompanied by ladies of the night wearing too much makeup and exposing too much chest. They were eating greedily, murmuring crude remarks to each other, and exchanging suggestive glances, anticipating the frolics to come.

Angèle had chosen a cassolette of andouillette with camembert, and Jenny was having langoustine ravioli with foie gras sauce. Anything could be had during the Occupation if you could pay for it. Restrictions and ration cards could be circumvented. Restaurant owners used all sorts of schemes to stock their kitchens.

Angèle didn't know that her new friend would be paying the bill with a tiny part of the 50,000 francs Jean de Dieu had retrieved from Prince Antonio's safe. He and Jenny wanted to make an impression on her. With her second glass of champagne, she began to relax. She suggested that Jenny must have a filthy rich German in her bed to be able to pay for such an outing. Jenny lied, saying she was servicing a high-ranking officer, very high-ranking indeed. Angèle raised an eyebrow, hoping for a name. But Jenny only said she could introduce her to someone just as high-ranking and loaded with dough.

Her new friend was delighted with this proposal. She toasted the rich lover she would be meeting. But why her? Was this just a stroke of luck or something else? Jenny answered that Angèle had been recommended. Someone in the Sphinx appreciated her work. The answer seemed to satisfy her. Jenny added quietly that there was still a small problem to be solved. She leaned in close and, feigning concern, reminded Angèle that she already had Baumeister. Oh, that penny pincher! Except for rare evenings at the cinema, he preferred unsophisticated eateries and sauerkraut with garlic. "Just imagine his breath," she exclaimed.

Jenny clinched her argument by mentioning that lately her lover had taken her to the Lido and the Folies Bergères. Before that, it had been the Casino de Paris and the Moulin de la Galette. Of course, it was all lies to entice Angèle. Speaking in a low voice, Angèle disparaged her lover further, saying his sexual demands were becoming more and more perverted. For her part, Jenny reported that her important German officer, who had been awarded the Iron Cross, fell asleep promptly after his basic needs were satisfied.

Jenny got to the heart of the matter at dessert, a chocolate praline tart for Angèle and a salted butter caramel éclair for her. Angèle listened attentively to her new friend's proposal. "Iron Cross" wanted to get rid of the major and put his own protégé in his place. Since they were all Germans, a bullet to the head was not an option. But blackmail would be a way to get him to resign. Would she be able to help? "Iron Cross" would compensate her for her efforts and introduce her to another Nazi hero, who would take her out to the Lapérouse and the Ritz. Angèle did not hesitate. For some time now she had been thinking about dumping her lover. And who better to replace him than a moneybags who fornicated without much imagination? The matter was settled, and Jenny, who had barely touched her champagne, ordered digestifs to wash down the meal.

As she walked back with Angèle, who lived close by, Jenny explained what was expected of her. She would invite the major to her place and get him to undress in dim light. Then, pretending to go to the bathroom, she would unlock the front door. Jenny would slip in and take some unforgettable photos. "Don't worry, I'll avoid taking any that show your face," she added. "He's the one I'm interested in."

Angèle promised to contact her when the Nazi was coming. To make sure she acted promptly, Jenny gave her 250 francs and promised the same amount again once she had taken the photos. "Iron Cross" was counting on her, she added as she was leaving.

Pierrette Doesn't Give In Easily

Baumeister had Pierrette brought to his office immediately after her arrest. During the first two hours of interrogation, he was firm but patient. "We know that Prince Antonio, the suspect in a case my men are working on, has made regular bank transfers to you." Could she tell him what they were for?

The woman acted innocent at first. She didn't know anything. She was an honest businesswoman and had the papers required for her hairdressing salon.

The major didn't like the way she was evading his questions. He decided to show her the document on his desk. It was a bank statement, identical to one that she had at home with her financial records.

Pierrette asked if he could lend her a magnifying glass because the type was too small for her eyes. The Nazi humoured her, ordering Lukas Betz to bring her one, and even a cup of coffee, real coffee, of course. It took the lieutenant half an hour to come back with a magnifying glass. Apparently, none of the investigators had one. The truth was that no one wanted to lend theirs. Baumeister had a reputation for not returning things. No one dared ask him to give anything back.

During the wait, the Nazi observed this Frenchwoman who appeared to have nothing to feel guilty about. She was facing a high-ranking member of the Gestapo who was pacing up and down like a caged lion in front of her, but she didn't seem perturbed. No beads of sweat on her forehead, no trembling, not even a stutter in her answers.

He remained silent to let her stew. Then, when she examined the bank document, she acted as if things were coming back to her. Yes, of course, now she remembered. He was that charming Black gentleman to whom she sold coal for the winter.

The major had been expecting such an answer. He summoned his lieutenant. "What did you see during your brief examination of the premises, Lieutenant Betz?"

"A hairdressing salon," said the young man. And upstairs he had found an illegal nursery. He had counted three young children and an infant, little beds, a playpen, diapers, and a kitchenette where a nanny was preparing baby bottles.

"Any coal?"

"No coal."

Baumeister put on a scandalized look. "Aren't you ashamed of yourself, Madame Pierrette? Lying to the Gestapo!" He played with his monocle, spinning it at the end of its cord, and Pierrette wondered if he was going to throw it at her.

Actually, she admitted, she wasn't the one selling the coal. She cashed the cheques from the African prince because the coal seller didn't have a bank account. She was doing a favour for a friend.

"Which friend? I want his name immediately. Write it down."

When she had written the name, Pierrette asked if she could be driven back to her salon.

"Not so fast," snapped the Nazi. Her statement would have to be checked. Once his men confirmed what she had said, he would give the order to have her returned home.

She drank her coffee and gave a deep sigh, annoyed.

The German officer, surprised that she had not yet shown the least sign of fear, commended her courage. "You've got guts, Madame. I hope for your sake that your statement will be corroborated. Otherwise, you're in danger of losing everything. Your beautiful teeth as well as your hairdressing salon."

The threat didn't have much effect.

Just then, Magda came in with a letter, and things started to become clear to the major. The letter was from a police commissioner, requesting that he show mercy to his cousin, the hairdresser, who was of French birth and would never collaborate with enemies of the Third Reich. It could only have been a misunderstanding, blah, blah, blah.

Baumeister didn't read the rest of the message. He crumpled it up, threw it into the wastebasket under his desk, and ordered Magda to do a "4-24."

That was code for opening an investigation of this police commissioner who dared to contact him without following the proper bureaucratic procedure. The letter altered the balance of power with Pierrette. Baumeister decided that a Frenchwoman who believed herself to be protected by a police commissioner had better find out who the true masters were in France. "Put her in cell C-4," he ordered his lieutenant. That was a narrow cage beside the torture room.

For five hours, Pierrette heard the cries of men and women being beaten and abused. She tried to keep calm. She covered her ears. She visualized the face of Suzy's little boy. That child must not be killed. He had become like a grandson to her. She prayed several times, asking the Good Lord for guidance. But the voices of the torture victims invaded her thoughts. Whenever a prisoner lost consciousness, she heard a bucket of water being thrown at him to revive him. She was next door to hell, and the major was the devil. It had been a total of seven hours since she had left her hairdressing salon and she didn't know when she would get back there. If only she could block out the cries of the people being tortured, she would be able to think and assess her situation.

After eight hours of detention, Baumeister had Pierrette released from her cell. She found herself once again facing the Nazi, who was staring at her with his monocle in his right eye. He decided to adopt a friendly tone. "We've checked, my dear Madame. Your friend does indeed sell coal illegally. But he doesn't know Prince Antonio. Besides, it's been three months since he last spoke to you. You know what I do to liars? I beat the soles of their feet until they're unable to walk for the rest of their lives."

Pierrette tried to answer, but stuttered. It was hot in this office and the handcuffs were chafing her wrists. She knew that the major was not making idle threats. Her hands trembling, she begged him to stop haranguing her. She had held out eight hours against a professional torturer, and she hoped Suzy and Rodolfo had made good use of that time. The moans of the torture victims were still ringing in her ears. More than anything, she wanted to avoid being tortured herself. "I'll tell you everything, Major. Promise me you won't send me down to the basement again."

"It all depends on what you say. Your life is in my hands. I can put a bullet between your eyes right here or just turn you over to my men in the basement, it'll take their minds off things having an old woman to play with. They're not picky."

She gulped, which made her cough. Baumeister remained impassive, his arms crossed over his round belly.

"For months I received cheques from Prince Antonio for taking care of his son in the nursery. The mother is one of my employees, Suzy."

The major blanched, suddenly realizing he had missed a key person in his search for the Angolan prince's diamonds.

"Suzy who?" he asked in an expressionless voice.

"Suzy Lazowski."

And a Jewess to boot, he thought. "Was she in the hairdressing salon when they picked you up?"

"Yes. Like every day of the week. She's my employee."

"What time does she finish?"

She looked at the office clock and answered, "In less than an hour."

He shouted to his lieutenant, "Put her back in cell C-4."

"No! I'm begging you."

"You thought you were going to intimidate me with your cousin the police commissioner, eh? That's why you were resisting. But your cousin is a doormat under my feet! There's no way he can help you. I'm the only one who can save your life!"

That was how Pierrette learned that her cousin had come forward. But, judging by the major's decision, it only added fuel to the fire.

"I swear to you, I never told him where I was. I didn't have a chance."

"Lieutenant, take this old bat away."

"Please! I'll do anything you want!"

The major let those words echo in his office. It was the sound of victory. Of his victory. No one could resist him. It had taken eight hours with this fat old lady simply because she had deluded herself with the notion of a policeman cousin rushing to her rescue. He had destroyed that illusion, had taken the hairdresser to the antechamber of horror and let her stew. And she had given in. She had waved the white flag.

"Anything?"

"Yes, anything."

"Okay. We'll take you to see our artist so he can make a composite sketch of that Suzy."

Relieved not to have to go back to the basement, she thanked him again and again.

"You'll give us her address. If you lie to me, you'll end up behind bars in Fresnes. I can promise you'll lose those extra kilos in prison."

He motioned for Magda to take her away. Lieutenant Betz was about to go with them.

"No. You stay here."

The lieutenant didn't like his boss's tone. It did not bode well.

"When I sent you to get Pierrette, what did I say was your mission?"

"To check out the place and give you a verbal report on what I saw."

"You didn't notice a Black child in the nursery? A little boy with dark skin? With African hair? Do you know what a Black looks like? Have you ever seen a chimpanzee? Have you ever gone to a zoo? I know you can't stand jazz, that music of savages. But your innocent eyes still must have seen a monkey in a zoo?"

The lieutenant didn't know what to answer. He remained at attention, stunned by his boss's verbal assault. "Yes, now that you mention it, Major, there was a Black child. There are so many of them in Paris, I didn't make the connection."

"Let me remind you that our suspects are Black!" The German officer scowled and the monocle dropped from his eye. "Go to the hairdressing salon and pick up this Suzy Lazowski! Maybe she's dumb enough to think we're questioning her boss for something else. And send some men to check her home. Seize anything important, such as identity papers, train schedules, or tickets. That woman is the girlfriend of the Angolan prince. She must know something about his diamonds."

The lieutenant gave his Hitler salute and left without waiting for the major to do likewise. Furious at being reprimanded, he considered asking for an immediate transfer. However, something made him decide to wait. He wanted to get to the bottom of this business with the Blacks, the jazzmen, and a Jewess who fornicated with a degenerate. This would be a story to tell at dinners with the Nazified Norwegian nobility when he was transferred.

Jenny Reports to Jean de Dieu

Jean de Dieu recognized Jenny's knock on his door. Two very quiet taps. He had to be listening closely to know she was there. He climbed out of his bathtub, which was so short he had to bend his knees to get his feet in, put on a bathrobe, and opened the door.

She was surprised by his appearance. "Oh, I see you were taking a bath."

"I was just at Prince Antonio's girlfriend's apartment and I burned some photos and other documents in her stove. The smell was clinging to my skin."

Jenny didn't comment. She was wearing the dress from her dinner with Angèle. A beautiful silk dress in a vaguely oriental style. She walked into the bathroom and took the dress off, keeping her slip on. She took the pitcher of hot water and poured it into the bath, which was starting to cool. Jean de Dieu enjoyed the moment of closeness with her. His difficult, risky day was ending auspiciously. She put more water on the stove to heat.

In the living room, the radio, tuned to a station in England, was playing "Body and Soul," recorded by saxophonist Coleman Hawkins in 1939. In spite of the static and low volume, the soft melody lent a special intimacy to the atmosphere.

They moved into the bedroom and Jenny made herself comfortable on the bed. As was his habit, Jean de Dieu brought out a culinary surprise. This time, it was an onion soup he had made, with lardons from a butcher who kept some aside for a select clientele. With it they shared a few slices of country bread.

She gave him her report on the meeting with Angèle. Then she put the tray down on the bedroom floor.

"When she tells you to come, I'll go there and take the photos," he said.

"No," said Jenny, "I'd rather do it myself."

Surprised, he looked her in the eye. "It's way too risky. "

She smiled wryly. "There you go again, acting like I matter to you."

"Stop it, Jenny. You know I care about you."

"I can stop the prostitution," she said. "Just for you."

He took her face in his hands and made her look at him. "No man or woman should tell you what to do, Jenny. Your freedom is the most precious thing there is. It's what I want, but it's your decision to make."

"Do you love me?"

Jean de Dieu's gave her a long kiss. "Yes, I love you. I have for months. But I didn't want you to think I was only interested in your body."

She snuggled against his shoulder. "I'm going to stop. Give me a little time. I've stopped before, you know. And then when the Germans arrived, it became difficult to earn a living importing Chinese curios. I can't be a waitress or a vendor in the market. I tried that. People mimic my accent. It's impossible. You don't mind me continuing? Tell me the truth."

"No. I know you're going to stop. I don't doubt it."

Jean de Dieu took a Leica camera out of the drawer of his bedside table. It was relatively small and easy to conceal. He handled it with surprising ease and Jenny could see he knew something about photography. He screwed and unscrewed the lens to show her how to go about it. He opened the bottom of the camera by turning a little handle. Then he took a small canister and a pair of scissors out of the drawer. The canister contained a roll of film. He trimmed the end and inserted it in the camera. Jenny watched him without saying a word.

He explained how to use the Elmar lens for close-ups. She repeated what he said to make sure she had understood properly. Their hands brushed against each other. They gazed at one another in lustful silence. Jean de Dieu put away the camera and kissed Jenny passionately. They ended up making love, forgetting the lit candles.

But in the middle of the night, Jean de Dieu had a nightmare and Jenny had to wake him up. "It was just a bad dream, Jean de Dieu."

"I'd been picked up by the Gestapo. They were about to shoot me."

Jenny reassured him, saying he had nothing to fear. She wiped his forehead with a handkerchief and went and got him a glass of water. "It's better to be beaten to death than to die of fright. That's a Chinese proverb," said Jenny.

"It's true," agreed her lover. "But they haven't got us yet."

She stroked his face and said, "Your fear only comes out in the night. In the daytime, you have nerves of steel."

He didn't answer. He was already asleep again.

Hans Solves a Problem for Armando

Prince Antonio was expecting Armando to call to let him know that Suzy and the child were in a safe place. The café on Rue Champollion was still closed. The blinds were drawn. Nothing could be seen from the outside. The owner seemed to be late opening his business. Hans and Jean de Dieu were supposed to meet him there. But it was only Hans who came. He entered through the secret door in the back. Armando welcomed him warmly and gave him a cup of his famous Brazilian hot chocolate.

"Where's Jean de Dieu?" asked Hans.

"I don't know," answered Armando. "He told me on the phone that he had to lose two guys who seemed to be following him in the métro."

"Ah," said Hans. He asked why the café was still closed.

"I'm afraid the police from the other day will come back today. That would be the third time. I gave them your names, Kassoma and Montlouis. They didn't find anything, of course. It's impossible to track down an address, an entry visa, or even a parking ticket in your names. So they've been harassing me."

"Do you want help?"

The proposal made Armando pause for a few seconds. What kind of help was Hans talking about? He knew him. That guy wouldn't hesitate. He thought for a moment and concluded, "No, I think I can handle them."

Hans shrugged. "Okay."

He waited for Armando to make the call to Prince Antonio. However, his friend remained seated, pensive.

"The boss is waiting for our call. If you don't call him, I'll do it myself."

"Okay. I was thinking that Jean de Dieu should be here."

"It's time."

Hans was right. If they didn't call at the exact time, the prince would conclude that the mission to rescue Suzy and the child had failed. Armando reached Prince Antonio quickly and delivered a banal message about the weather. Their boss replied using a code familiar to the Brazilian, saying that things were progressing for his return to Paris.

At the end of that very short call, someone knocked on the front door. Armando signaled to Hans to keep quiet. He walked across the café, turned on the ceiling light, and opened the door. The sound of the door chime was accompanied by familiar voices. Hans recognized those of the two police officers from the last time. They entered, slamming the door behind them.

Hans, in the back room, took out his 9 mm ivory-grip Luger. Without making a sound, he took the silencer from the lining of his coat where he'd hidden it and screwed it onto the barrel of the pistol. He went and stood near the secret door with his back to the wall. He had to be ready for anything.

"Armando, my dear friend," said the policeman playing good cop. "Do you have news for us?"

"Messieurs, I would have liked to give you more news. But Kassoma and Montlouis don't come here anymore. I think you've scared them off."

The officer playing bad cop raised his voice. "This is the third time we've come to see you. Tell us what you know. Or else we'll take you in and I don't know if your wife will recognize you once we're finished with you."

"I don't know anything! I've told you everything!"

Hans heard a scream. Armando had fallen to the floor.

"Filthy Brazilian! You want to play tough? We'll show you."

Hans entered the café from behind the two police officers. He saw the bigger one kick his friend in the ribs. "If I were you, I wouldn't do that."

The two police officers turned around at the same time. The smaller one, the one playing good cop, remained motionless, while the other one tried to draw his weapon. Hans aimed his pistol and put a bullet in his forehead with a muffled sound. The man dropped to the floor. The smaller one put his hands up. "Don't shoot. We can make a deal."

Armando was twisted with pain on the floor of his café.

"First of all, you're going to apologize to my friend," said Hans.

"Forgive me. We didn't mean to ..."

"Now say your prayers."

For a moment the policeman was speechless. This guy was going to kill him! "Wait. You can't just kill a cop. Two, even worse. I can fix things. I'll say it was an accident."

Armando stopped clutching his ribs and sat up to try to get to his feet. He heard the dull sound of the silencer and saw the second policeman drop on top of his dead colleague. "But..."

"Armando, no need to thank me for getting you out of a tough spot. Just tell me where we can hide the bodies."

Faced with a fait accompli, Armando stood up in silence. He realized things had taken a final, irrevocable turn. "Okay." He went out the secret door and checked that the coast was clear. They took the bodies to the Resistance member's place next door in a wheelbarrow covered with a tarp. The neighbour, a mailman, was at work. They left the corpses behind a knoll, covered with the tarp. At nightfall, Armando would bury them in the basement with the help of the neighbour. They would join a German soldier the neighbour had killed during a foot chase at dawn.

Returning to the café, they found Jean de Dieu there, smoking a Gauloise. He looked at them without a word, his hat tilted slightly and a smile on his lips. His friends didn't need to provide any explanation.

"You'd better clean up the place, Armando. Hans and I will move their car. Hans, do you think they followed you?"

"No, they had no idea I was here. That's how I got the drop on them."

"Nice work," said Jean de Dieu. Seeing Armando's uncertain expression, he took him by the shoulder. "Those guys would never have stopped. You'd have ended up six feet under."

"Another beautiful day to stay alive," said Hans, winking at Armando.

"Thanks for your help, Hans," said Armando, his eyes lowered. He immediately went to work to clean the floor and check the walls for blood splatters.

Hans and Jean de Dieu slipped out into the street without being noticed. They had no difficulty recognizing the policemen's car. It was parked right in front, illegally, and the smaller of the policemen had left his coat in it. You could see the handle of a gun sticking out of an outside pocket. Who but a cop could be so careless in a time of war? His coat collar turned up and his hat pulled down to his eyebrows, Hans forced the door open with a metal bar. When he heard the click of the lock, he nodded to Jean de Dieu.

Armando was watching them from the window. The boldness of those two never ceased to impress him. Weren't they afraid of getting caught? He went back to scrubbing the floor to erase any traces of what had happened in his café.

Hans and Jean de Dieu didn't move the car very far. They abandoned it near the Odéon métro station, a few minutes away. They had made sure to wear gloves so as not to leave prints in the vehicle.

The friends each took a different route back to the Renault, which was parked on Rue Racine. It was raining lightly in Paris, an icy rain, and people were running for cover.

Prince Antonio and the Shadows of Lisbon

Lisbon was being buffeted by winds from the Atlantic and its shoreline was being lashed by waves. Prince Antonio, famished, had left his apartment late in the day, wearing his leather gloves and carrying his ivory-headed cane. He was going to have dinner at a restaurant he was fond of. It was in his neighbourhood, the Baixa, and it was called O Peixe Vermelho, The Goldfish. He didn't need the métro or a taxi. The walk did him good, but above all, it allowed him to check if he was being followed. A few other people were out walking and were in no hurry to pass him. He was only able to make out silhouettes in the dim light, without being sure of anything.

Since he was a regular at O Peixe Vermelho, his table was waiting for him. It was in a corner from which he could see all the customers who came into the restaurant. He ate a dish called Bacalhau com Natas, cod in cream. It was baked in the oven with potatoes, milk, and grated cheese. He washed it down with an excellent vinho verde. Then he headed out, not without leaving a good tip and saying goodbye to the waiters. He buttoned his grey wool coat to the neck. The damp cold of the Lisbon winter chilled him to the bone. He knew that by next month the cold would be ebbing, and the almond and jasmine would be about to bloom. But they weren't there yet.

His footsteps resounded on the shiny white cobblestones. He heard other footsteps behind him. When he turned around, a man approached him. The man's eyes were hidden behind big dark glasses and he was wearing a black fedora and a black coat. "Would His Highness grant me a few minutes of his time?" he asked. His Portuguese was clear, with an accent that sounded Slavic to Prince Antonio.

The approach seemed courteous, but Prince Antonio knew he had to be on his guard. "To whom do I owe the honour?"

There were other people walking in the lighted lane leading to the prince's apartment. He barely slowed down. He didn't want to stop for a stranger.

"Excuse me. My name is Stan Patak and I've been sent by friends who wish you well."

The prince smiled and waited to hear more.

"You see, in these difficult times, we're worried about the future of humanity. Especially the oppressed peoples of Africa, such as your own people under Portuguese colonization. All peoples have a right to their freedom, is that not so? My friends are opposed to the exploitation of man by man. You know what I'm saying?"

"Mr. Patak, you approach me in the street to talk about friends of yours? I'm not interested in them. Tell them I have nothing to sell."

The mysterious stranger laughed, not at all discouraged by the prince's response. He took off his glasses, perhaps trying to appear more sincere. His pale grey eyes gave Prince Antonio goose bumps. "I understand your hesitation. Why would you risk talking to a stranger who accosts you in a Lisbon alley at dusk? In your place, I, too, would be hesitant." He adopted a confidential tone, looking into the prince's eyes. "My friends' aim is to free all oppressed peoples. They urge you to become a leader for the future of the Angolan people."

"I think you've got the wrong man. I don't want any part of that kind of thing. As the heir to the throne of the Kingdom of Kongo, I'll return home one day and lead my people, as my father does now. No more, no less."

The other man continued in a condescending tone of voice, "It is true that my friends see monarchies as obstacles to the development of peoples. That being said, they are ready to make concessions on this point, given your ability to penetrate the upper echelons of Portuguese power and cross borders unscathed." He glanced behind him, forcing Prince Antonio to do the same. All they saw was parents and their children returning home to their warm beds for a good night's sleep.

"You're being followed, Your Highness, and I'm not talking about me. You're what we call a potential source." He saw that Prince Antonio was shaking his head, refusing that term. "Or if you don't like that, you can be an *asset*, as the British say. Someone who helps without being part of any group in particular. After all, who can be against the right of self-determination of peoples? No one."

The prince took advantage of an opening into a poorly lit alley to grab the man and push him against a wall. With a quick twist of his wrist, he pulled a slender blade from inside his cane. It was about 10 centimetres long. "I'll let you walk away alive so you can go tell your friends that religion is not the opium of the people. But I'm tempted to leave you a souvenir on that pale, poorly shaven neck."

Pinned by the imposing strength of the young prince, the stranger was unable to move. His frightened eyes were fixed on the blade, which glinted even in the semi-darkness. His Adam's apple moved up and down two, then three times before he pleaded, "Forgive me, Your Highness. I won't bother you anymore."

The Angolan, who was a head taller than the Slav, glared at him with scorn and sheathed the blade in one quick movement. The man turned on his heel and ran, glancing back from time to time to make sure the prince wasn't following him. Prince Antonio understood that he was an agent of the NKVD, the intelligence and secret police agency of the Soviet Union. He would never collaborate with those Communists. The German-Soviet Non-Aggression Pact of 1939, which had been shattered by the German invasion in June 1941, was indicative of Stalin's duplicity. Prince Antonio was no Communist. He knew the fate Lenin had reserved for the Russian nobility and he did not intend to ally himself with beheaders of aristocrats.

He continued on his way home, dreading another unpleasant encounter. However, none occurred and he was able to get back to his apartment without further incident.

Jenny and the Photographs of Major Baumeister

Angèle was about to go powder her nose when her lover came through the door of her apartment in the 6th arrondissement. Usually Major Baumeister preferred to meet her at his residence, on Rue Dufrenoy. However, she had promised him she would be particularly shameless if he agreed to spend a few hours at her place. That was enough to convince him. He would bring a few "toys" with him to spice things up.

It was early in the evening. Paris was shrouded in a frigid fog and the Eiffel Tower was asleep, dimly lit so it couldn't be used as a landmark for war planes from London. The major set two bottles of champagne down on the table in Angèle's little dining room and went and locked the apartment door. The place was simply decorated. She didn't spend a lot of time there. But she had tried to make it feel more intimate for the occasion. She had softened the lighting with sheer yellow fabric over the lamps. She had even taken the trouble to scatter a few rose petals on the bed to add a romantic touch. Candles placed here and there allowed Baumeister to light a cigar that he had no intention of finishing.

As a preamble, Angèle performed a belly dance in her transparent lingerie. A gramophone bought at the flea market played oriental music. The sound hissed a little, but Baumeister was concentrating on his lover's gyrations. He enjoyed watching her hips sway while he savoured a glass of Moët & Chandon confiscated from a black marketeer. She followed the rhythm of the music, gazing at him languorously. The movements made his mouth water and he quickly unbuttoned his uniform. Handcuffs and a riding crop fell out of his pants pockets. The major acted as if he were discovering those objects for the first time and he laughed, already lightheaded from the champagne.

Once naked, he leaped onto the bed and planted long kisses on Angèle's full lips. When he tried to hold her still to put the handcuffs on her, she motioned to him to wait. She needed to go to the powder room. He shrugged and went to the dining room to get another bottle of champagne. He poured himself a glass. Angèle went into the bathroom, waited a few minutes for him to return to the bed, and on her way back unlocked the apartment door. She came back and lay down. The major was anticipating the delights to come.

Jenny, in a nearby café, had seen the German officer get out of his Mercedes and rush into Angèle's building. She finished her tea slowly to give them time to relax. Baumeister's driver, Hermann, did not stay, and she watched with satisfaction as the taillights of the Mercedes disappeared in the distance. She knew he would come back to pick up his boss and resolved to get out of the building before he showed up again. She checked one last time that she had the Leica with its retractable lens in the bag slung over her shoulder. She had dressed in a black blouse with a big collar and navy blue pants whose high waist flattered her figure, and whose wide legs would allow her to run if necessary. She was wearing tango dancer's shoes whose heels she had padded with a thin layer of velvet. It was not snowing. Her tweed coat, also black, went just to her knee. On her head she had a dark, puffy Gavroche cap.

She pulled down the visor of her hat and went into the building. She climbed the stairs in the dark without meeting a soul. At Angèle's door, she decided that her shoes were still making too much noise and left them beside the door after slipping inside. She heard the loud voice of the major giving his lover orders. But what was he demanding she do? After taking a few steps into the apartment, Jenny saw that the game consisted of having her kiss his toes. Which Angèle did after a little crack of the riding crop on her derrière. Jenny took out the camera and made sure the lens was locked in place. She remembered Jean de Dieu's warning: "If the lens is not seated properly, your photos will be blurry."

She crept to the bedroom door, which was half open. Angèle's bed was against the far wall. The major was facing the wall, his back to the door. Stretching a bit, Jenny, stayed close to the floor. She could see the major almost in profile, with the large protruding stomach his military uniform hid so well, the result of his frequent libations in the brasseries of Paris. Jenny took advantage of the drumbeats in the music to press the shutter button. Again and again. In the little viewfinder window, she saw his erection, his imperious expression, the crop in his hand. The silhouette of Angèle's behind remained in the shadows.

Baumeister accused Angèle of flirting with the clients at the Sphinx and let loose a string of insults. His mistress, in handcuffs, admitted that she lusted after men, that she was insatiable. This confession caused the major to curse in German. He jerked the handcuffs to force his lover to beg forgiveness. On the contrary, she laughed, shrugging her shoulders, which made her flesh tremble in the yellowish light. Her defiance increased the major's excitement. Jenny took another photo just when his crop struck Angèle's derrière, slightly harder than the first time. He hit her again. She begged his forgiveness and kissed his feet, then his knees, then his upper thighs, and finally, his erect member. Jenny got another shot with the major close to climax, sweating profusely, his eyes shut. He had unwittingly turned his head towards the lens. He pushed his lover onto the bed. She lay stretched out with her shackled hands above her head. The major freed one of her hands from the handcuffs so that she could use it to stroke him, and then he fastened the handcuffed hand to the headboard. He got up out of the bed and Jenny instinctively crept back. Then he went around the bed to the other side, passing closer to the lens without realizing it. Caught up in the passion of the moment, he didn't imagine that there was a woman lying on the floor in the dim light aiming the lens of a camera at him as he was framed against the half-open door. Jenny pressed the shutter button of the Leica again.

Satisfied with her work, she slowly backed away, still crawling. This was not easy, because she had the camera in one hand and the pair in the bed were silent. She froze in panic for a few seconds when the major started to get up to serve himself more champagne. Angèle held him back and offered to serve him "like a king" while he regained his strength. Baumeister freed her, and she walked past Jenny without looking at her, the handcuffs swinging from one wrist. It was dark and Jenny, as still as a cat, didn't look up. Angèle came back with the other bottle of champagne and served the major a big glass, a smile on her lips. Jenny noticed the redness of Angèle's buttocks and she didn't envy her.

Jenny tiptoed towards the apartment door. All that champagne had made the major want to go to the bathroom. Hearing him stand up, Jenny slipped behind the coat rack by the door. There were several winter garments on it, including the major's heavy coat, which smelled of cigars. Jenny held her breath as the major passed. He went into the bathroom without noticing anything. While he was emptying his bladder, Jenny left the camouflage of coats and moved to the door like a shadow. She picked up her shoes and went down the stairs without making a sound.

On his way back to the bedroom, the major noticed that the apartment door was unlocked. He thought he had been careless. How could he have forgotten to lock it? No, he vaguely remembered that he had. The champagne was making him doubt his behaviour. Had he locked it? He checked behind the coats, then glanced around the little living room. Nothing. There was no one there. Satisfied, he locked the door properly and returned to Angèle, who was ready to serve him.

Baumeister went on to a second session, including more insults, more threats, and more lashes with the crop. An hour later, he left the building and got into his Mercedes, with Hermann holding the door for him.

Suzy Is Worried about Her Boss

Jean de Dieu was at Armando's with Nadège, as well as Suzy and her little boy. Suzy was worried about her boss. Jean de Dieu had said Pierrette hadn't returned home, and that she was in Fresnes Prison for breaking the Law on the Status of Jews. One of his informants had confirmed it.

This news was discouraging to Suzy, and she felt guilty. Jean de Dieu tried to reassure her, saying her boss would be freed soon. Nadège, smiling and friendly, tried to distract everyone with little homemade cakes. "Come now, everything will be fine," she said. "You're safe here. And so is Rodolfo." She tickled the chubby-cheeked toddler, who responded with a big smile.

"Thank you," said Suzy, embarrassed for complaining, when she and her child would certainly have been detained had it not been for her new friends. "I don't know where I'd be without you."

Jean de Dieu was sure that Pierrette had talked. A woman in her fifties could not hold out against the Gestapo for twenty-four hours. Maybe seven or eight hours if she was brave. The most determined people in the resistance cracked in two or three days or died from exhaustion and torture. You could count the ones who held out a week on the fingers of one hand. But what did Pierrette know? She knew Suzy's address and her family name, and she knew of her relationship with Prince Antonio. Jean de Dieu figured that the Nazis were hoping an informer would rat the Jewish woman out. He had to act before that happened.

Jean de Dieu's Revenge

Jean de Dieu had again managed to obtain the services of Philippe the carpenter, Matty's brother-in-law. For 200 francs, Philippe was to deliver an urgent letter addressed to Major F. Baumeister at the Hôtel Majestic. To make sure he looked credible, Armando had borrowed the uniform of his friend the mailman who was in the Resistance. The uniform was a bit snug because of the carpenter's stocky build. That didn't keep him from going to the Majestic and making the delivery.

The carpenter passed a group of soldiers, machine guns on their hips, standing under three huge red and white banners with big swastikas on them. He showed his fake postal worker's identity card. It was the mailman's card with Philippe's photo and a false name. A soldier searched him and let him pass without paying too much attention to the document. He saw mailmen every day and everything seemed to be in order. Inside, on a platform in the centre, there was a large counter with a wicket. The place was swarming with soldiers and officers going about their business. Some were having a heated discussion in front of a map of the city, others were getting on or off the elevators. The clatter of typewriters resounded from the adjoining rooms. The German soldier behind the wicket looked up and waited for the phony mailman to speak.

"Urgent letter."

The soldier motioned to Philippe to pass him the letter. He read the name of the recipient and saw the "Urgent" stamp and immediately grabbed the telephone and dialed the number for Baumeister's office. Philippe waited for him to sign a paper confirming receipt of the letter. When the call was over, the soldier initialed the paper and Philippe left the hotel, fighting the urge to run. His heart was pounding, but he was hiding his emotion well.

Once he was out of that snake pit, he slung his bag over his right shoulder, and Hans, seeing this signal from a distance, went to a post office and telephoned Armando to say in their code that the mission had been accomplished.

Magda came down from the third floor to pick up the letter marked "Urgent." She exchanged a smile with the young man at reception, who was turning on the charm. Maybe she would agree to go for a drink with him one of these days. It would be terrible to be in such a romantic city and not take advantage of it. The major made her work like a dog. But she shouldn't complain. Lieutenant Betz was his whipping boy, not her. If she were in his place, she would have asked for a transfer long ago.

In fact, Lukas Betz was in his superior's office when Magda returned. He had incurred the major's wrath for finding Suzy's apartment empty of any identity papers. The burned remains of her photos were among the ashes in her little stove. The secretary listened at the door, glad there was someone who had it worse than she did.

She put the letter down on her desk. These letters marked "Urgent" were often from famished informers, accusing neighbours or family members in hope of a crust of bread. They didn't know that the major did not concern himself with petty criminals, small fry, as he liked to say. Ration card thieves or people carrying fake war veterans' identity cards were of little interest to him. Magda suspected that this letter would end up in the hands of subordinates on the first floor, where she also had a few admirers.

She opened the envelope absent-mindedly, a lump in her throat. She hadn't chosen a military career to live a life of abstinence. She sighed wearily, filled with a desire for romance.

The sight of the first photograph dispelled any feelings of longing. She recognized the major, stark naked, the riding crop in his hand. She immediately turned the photo over, her face flushed with horror. But that was only the beginning. There were three other photos. Baumeister, his eyes closed, revelling in fellatio. Then another, and another. There was no doubt that it was the major. However, his companion remained in the shadows. There was a typed note in the envelope. After turning the photos over to shield them from inquisitive eyes, Magda read the message: "Major, we intend to send these lovely photos to collaborationist papers like *Je suis partout* and *Paris-Soir* as well as to members of the Resistance, who will no doubt plaster these images all over Paris. Free Pierrette, the owner of the hairdressing salon, immediately or you will be totally humiliated."

Magda put the photos back in the envelope, panic-stricken. What should she do? Give those pictures to the major in person? He would subject her to his tyrannical wrath even though she had had nothing to do with them. Somebody else, a man, would have to show him these images. At that very moment, Lieutenant Betz came out of his boss's office, visibly annoyed. Magda realized that this was her opportunity to get rid of a hot potato. "Lieutenant Betz?"

Betz turned and frowned. He was about to give her the brush-off. A secretary should know when to address an officer. This was not the time. But he saw her pallor and heard her faltering voice. This young woman who was always so sure of herself must have had a shock. His attitude changed. "What's the matter, Magda?'

She handed him the envelope, her eyes lowered. "I don't know what to do with this."

The young officer figured it was a letter from some jilted lover of Magda's. At the sight of the first photo, his eyes almost popped out of their sockets. He blinked, not sure whether to believe what he was seeing. He glanced at Magda, who was still looking down at the floor, embarrassed. After reading the message, he took a deep breath. "Okay," he said. "I'll take care of it."

"Thank you," she replied. She went and sat down behind her typewriter, happy for once that it was so huge. She could keep her head down and avoid the lieutenant's eyes.

"Magda?"

What does he want with me now? she wondered. "Yes, Lieutenant Betz?"

"How did you get this letter?"

"The mailman brought it. I got a call from reception and I went downstairs."

"How many people have seen these photos?"

"You and I, Lieutenant," she replied in a low voice.

The young officer realized that she understood the importance of keeping the photos confidential. He examined the images intently. Magda could see him out of the corner of her eye, and she wondered why he was so curious. Lukas Betz chose one of the photos, the most incriminating one, and slipped it into his pants pocket.

Magda didn't understand what he was up to. What was he going to do with that photo? Was he a pervert? Could the rumours about him be true? At any rate, he had never shown any interest in her, and she had turned many men's heads. One day, the major himself had even put his hand on her bum and said, "Don't worry, Magda, Lukas Betz is harmless."

The lieutenant knocked on his boss's door.

"Come in!" Baumeister looked up and saw that it was his subordinate. "Ah, it's you."

Betz did not perform the Hitler salute, and Baumeister immediately felt anxious. Something wasn't right. Usually, that young man didn't miss an opportunity. Why this change? "Is there a problem?"

The lieutenant, as solemn as a judge, put the envelope down on the desk in front of the major, who eyed it suspiciously. Even the way Lukas had put the envelope down was new. The gesture seemed bold, even teasing.

"What is this letter?"

The young man didn't reply. He stared at the wall behind his boss. "I can't tell you, Major. You'll have to see for yourself."

Baumeister grabbed the envelope impatiently to check what was in it. The message fell out first. He read it quickly. Images? Newspapers? What was going on? His pulse quickened when he took out the photos. There were three there. Three images that were like bombs going off in his head. He spat out a curse and moved his chair back as if the photos were going to catch fire and burn his face. "Where did you get this?" he asked gruffly. He glared at Betz, his gaze murderous, his fists clenched on his desk. The three stacks of files were in front of him. The yellow stack for verification on the left, the brown one, the promising cases, in the middle, and the red one, arrests and results of interrogations, on the right. But he didn't see them anymore.

"The mailman." Betz replied. "Magda went to pick up the mail on the ground floor."

"Who opened the envelope?"

To protect the young woman, Lieutenant Betz lied. "I did. Magda gave it to me. Since it was marked urgent, she passed it on to me."

So the well-bred young man was trying to protect the young lady in distress. A pathetic lie, thought the major. "Of course," he replied, and noted, "There's no return address."

Betz realized the major was playing for time. He wanted to know if he could count on his subordinate's discretion. The young man decided to take the initiative. "You can count on my silence, Major. I am at your service and my loyalty to you knows no bounds." He finally performed the Hitler salute, clicking his heels, staring into space.

What a fool, thought Baumeister. Even dumber than I thought. In his place, I would have run straight to General von Bose. "Very good, Lieutenant. I must admit I underestimated you. You've put Germany's honour above trivial considerations. You have the mettle of the Aryan warrior "

The young man remained in his position with his arm raised, like an Apollo of ancient Rome.

"Know that for the honour of the Third Reich, this letter deserves my consideration." The major gestured to Betz to lower his arm and take a seat facing him. Meanwhile, he reread the message in silence. Each photo was like a hammer blow to his temples. He wanted to murder this blackmailer. His hands were trembling with rage. His monocle slipped out because of the sweat on his face. He wiped his forehead. His words cut through the deadly silence like a cleaver. "Free Pierrette."

"Major, if you'll permit, we can track down the culprit. If we activate all our Paris informants, we can find the source of the message in less than twenty-four hours, before the next issues of the newspapers come out."

"Free her," Baumeister repeated with unusual calm.

Betz insisted, in a softer voice, almost a whisper, "The mailman, Major. We can find him by contacting the central post office."

The major turned red with rage and shouted, "Do you actually think it was a real mailman? Look at the cancellation of the stamp, it's a fake. The date was tampered with." Seeing the lieutenant's stunned expression, the major added, "Yes, Lieutenant Betz. An imposter came into the Hôtel Majestic and outwitted the guards. Now, go free the Frenchwoman. Apologize to her on my behalf and have my driver take her home in my Mercedes. A bureaucratic error that won't happen again. The case is closed. Hurry up."

Betz insisted on saluting again and Baumeister clenched his fists to keep from shouting at him to stop his carrying on. But he managed to restrain himself, and the young man left to go to Fresnes Prison.

The major left his office after Betz and asked Magda for a coffee. The young woman seemed to have shrunk a few centimetres. He could hardly see her head behind the typewriter.

"Right away, Major."

Angèle Is on the Hot Seat

Angèle was summoned to the major's apartment that very evening. His Mercedes and driver were waiting for her in front of her building. For the first time, the vehicle looked to her like a hearse. How was she going to get out of the clutches of this professional torturer? Jenny had paid her well, even a little too well, and she had no intention of selling her out. It wasn't a matter of heroism. She knew that if she made the slightest confession, she would be signing her own death warrant. She had been sleeping with Baumeister long enough to be aware of his cold heart, his total lack of remorse or empathy. He was only happy when he was causing pain.

She pulled herself together on the stairway leading to the major's apartment. A little powder on her nose, a fresh coat of lipstick, and a misting of the perfume he adored, Sweet Bambou by Weil.

The major was still wearing his uniform, and the lights seemed to be on in all the rooms of the apartment. Not the time or place for romance. He barely smiled, gave her a perfunctory kiss when she held out her cheek to him, and pointed to a chair across from the couch. Then he stared at her like a predator, a cigar in his hand.

"You got me, didn't you. Go on, tell me the truth."

No preamble? she thought. This was serious. "What are you talking about?" she asked as if she were completely dumbfounded. She was a good actress. Very good. You had to be to sell your body. She feigned bewilderment.

He told her what he had found in his mail at the office. She acted scandalized. She opened her eyes wide, opened her mouth, shocked. She said she was outraged, even offended, that he could think for a single instant that she could have had anything to do with such a distasteful scheme. She had already said "my love" three times since she'd started speaking, and her eyes were filling with tears, which she wiped away before they could spoil her make-up.

The situation was not to Baumeister's advantage. As a professional interrogator, he knew setting was very important in obtaining a confession. The basement at his workplace, cell C-4, would have been the perfect environment. Angèle would have confessed quickly. However, the lady of the evening could not be seen at the Majestic or in any other Gestapo office. His taking her to restaurants and shows was tolerated. But for her to go from paramour to suspect would surely earn him a summons to General von Bose's office. His flawless reputation as a torturer would be ruined. He could already imagine the rumours. Baumeister had been taken in by a prostitute. She had pulled a fast one on him. "The door to the apartment was unlocked when I went to the bathroom. Did you do it?"

She denied it, shaking her head, saddened that he should suspect her. "Pull yourself together, my darling. I'm the one who loves you. And you're forgetting one thing, I'm a victim here too. You think that because of my occupation I don't mind being secretly photographed? How little you know me. I too have my pride."

She was on the attack. Her arsenal was holding up well and her performance as a wronged woman was worthy of applause. Angèle knew she was playing for keeps. Playing for her life. She realized the major was trying to penetrate her charade. However, in this apartment, she didn't panic. Behind them was the dining table that had already served for playful lovemaking. Farther on, the bedroom with its four-poster bed that had creaked under the major's thrustings. No, this place of pleasure could not be the place of confession.

"You're not the victim. I'm the one who was the target. Do you know what an 'Aunt Minnie' is?"

"No, I have no idea."

"It's a photograph that shows only the elements of interest for intelligence purposes. The person in the foreground is out of focus. You're

'Aunt Minnie' in those photos. You were spared. That's how I know you were in on it."

He had played his trump card, but Angèle was not flustered. This was a matter of life and death for her, and she did not intend to let a word of confession slip from her mouth. She threw herself at his feet and pressed her chest to his knees. "My love, if you think it was me, I would rather die," she said, her voice breaking. "Do whatever you want with me."

He pushed her away and she fell back. Her dress lifted and he could see her underwear.

She raised herself onto her knees and took hold of his pant leg. "I love you and you know it! I'm ready to die for you," she cried, in a scene worthy of an acting award. She put her hands together, "Handcuff me and take me to prison! I'll be your prisoner if you want! I'll be anything you want me to be, my darling! I'm innocent. I'll do whatever you desire."

He tried to shake her off his pant leg, but she held on tighter. Her cries and her weeping were starting to worry him. He couldn't have a scandal in this bourgeois building or he would have to explain himself to a German administrator who lived on the same floor.

"All right," he said, "I believe you. Stand up!"

She took her time, still sniffing to show her sorrow. Standing, she buttoned the bodice of her dress, which had been open, revealing her corset and her ample bosom. The major wasn't even looking. He was pacing his living room like a caged lion. Angèle went over to him and put her hand between his legs.

"Don't touch me! You filthy…" He didn't complete his insult, remembering that he had to keep his voice low.

Angèle backed away, upset. Without another word, she picked up her bag and headed for the door.

He caught up with her, grabbed her by the hair, and whispered in her ear, "I know you betrayed me but I can't prove it. At least, not yet. When I do, you're a dead woman!"

She didn't turn around. The major's words convinced her that she had to put some distance between him and herself.

She would have to wait some time before Jenny could introduce her to the Nazi general who would take her to the Ritz and Maxim's. Baumeister might be transferred in a few months, or in prison, or even dead. Who knew what fate had in store for a man like him? So she would be patient and lie low for several weeks, even several months. The people at the Sphinx would understand. In these times of war, the girls would come and go and then come back again.

Outside, Angèle walked past the Mercedes and the major's driver. She gave Hermann a triumphant look. After all, she had survived a torturer.

Lieutenant Lukas Betz Has His Limits

Lieutenant Betz's colleagues often said that a meeting with a general could make or break a career. He brooded for an hour or two before making the decision to report the major. Baumeister ridiculed his lack of battlefield experience with thinly veiled insults. The innuendos had begun as soon as he was assigned the position of the major's right-hand man. In addition, Betz was subjected to Baumeister's contempt for homosexuals, although he had never said he was one. His private life was his own business, after all. That didn't prevent the major from talking about his "doe eyes" that kept missing clues. The lieutenant knew that if he weren't the son of a highly placed industrialist, Baumeister would long ago have sent him to fight on the Eastern Front, hoping he would be killed. No, that man was dangerous and Lukas Betz was going to ruin his career with a sex scandal. An opportunity like this would not present itself twice.

The lieutenant was in the office of General Erich von Bose, a man in his early sixties with steely blue eyes, who had earned his highest distinctions in Poland. Indeed, there was a tactical defence that bore his name: the von Bose defence against enemy tanks. Yes, *that* general. He was reputedly destined for a great future. Rumour had it that Hitler reserved a chair for him at his side whenever he visited the Bavarian Alps. He was one of the officers welcomed in the Eagle's Nest on a rocky summit, where the Führer received his close collaborators.

Von Bose's manner was friendly, and he offered Betz coffee. His secretary, unlike Magda, was full-figured, and she was much older. Betz had gotten a five-minute appointment with the general by using the name of his father, the industrialist Klaus Betz, a long-time funder of the Nazi party. The secretary had immediately understood that she had to mention the father to von Bose. This young man who had leapfrogged over captains and colonels to contact the general directly must have an important reason or else he was crazy. One way or another, she had to convey his request to von Bose.

Sitting at his big walnut desk, the general took a sip of coffee and set his cup down in a saucer. The lieutenant, standing, consumed his coffee in one gulp and almost burned his throat. He wanted to put the cup down before his superior noticed his hand was shaking.

"I'm listening, Lieutenant." Von Bose glanced at his watch.

"It's about my immediate superior, Major Baumeister."

This wasn't a good beginning, thought the general. If this young man thought he had time to manage squabbles among colleagues, he'd put him on the next train to Berlin and assign him to menial duties.

Lukas Betz realized he lacked the tone of voice or the precise vocabulary to express what he wanted to say. So he took out the photo and placed it in front of the general. Then he took two steps back, his eyes lowered.

The major was easily recognizable in the photo, clutching a woman's buttocks. Von Bose swore and asked Betz the source of the photo.

Betz explained that Magda had shown him several photos. He recounted the conversation he had had with the major. Anticipating the general's question, he added that no one had laid eyes on those photos apart from Magda, Baumeister, himself, and now, the general.

"Thank you for coming directly to me. I know your father, he can be proud of your tact and your prompt action. Right now, I would ask you to act as if nothing has happened. I will talk to the major."

Betz was about to say something more, but it was the general's turn to anticipate. "No, I won't mention your name. Baumeister won't know that I got this photo from you. Dismissed."

Betz gave his smartest Hitler salute and turned around. He had a deep, pleasurable feeling of having gotten his revenge. He was very angry with that fat slob Baumeister for making him his whipping boy. All the thinly veiled insults about his bourgeois origins and the barbs about homosexuality were soon going to stop.

When the secretary saw him emerge from the office with more assurance than when he arrived, she was filled with admiration for the young officer. There's a guy who has guts, she said to herself.

Suzy Is in Danger Again

Armando had called a meeting at his place. There were Jean de Dieu, Suzy, Nadège, and Hans, who arrived last, his face hidden under a hat pulled down over his eyes. The toddler was asleep in his mother's lap. It must have been about eleven at night. Armando was talking in a low voice. He didn't want to wake the child, but above all, he didn't want the neighbours to know that there was a meeting going on.

In recent days, tenants on the floor above had asked if he had visitors. They had heard noise, in particular a baby crying. Armando apologized profusely for not having warned them. He said his wife's cousin Isabelle was visiting with her child. Just a short visit before they returned to the Morbihan, in Brittany, he lied.

The friends looked at each other in silence. They understood that Suzy had to leave shortly. An extended visit could arouse suspicion and lead to someone informing on them.

Nadège turned to her husband and said, "We can have her sleep in the old lady's apartment. She has a spare room."

Armando explained to the others, "We take care of an old woman who lives in the apartment at the end of the hallway. Madeleine is no longer in her right mind, but she refuses to go to an old-age home. She's waiting for her son Alexandre, who's in the Resistance. She lives alone with her cat. We do her shopping, we wash her dishes and her clothes. She often pees her pants. We make sure she has what she needs.

Armando had known his neighbour Alexandre well. The bachelor in his thirties had cared lovingly for his mother. A café waiter with a smile always on his lips, always ready to help. But when the Germans came to Paris, Alexandre changed. He became taciturn and secretive, and in the summer of 1941, he decided to take up arms. He had entrusted his mother to Armando on the eve of his departure to join the Resistance. "But don't tell her I'm going to fight, that would break her heart," he had said. "I'm asking you to take care of her because you're a good, decent man." Armando, faced with a fait accompli, had agreed to look after her with Nadège's help. He would never abandon his wife and undertake a suicidal mission. He wouldn't hurt a fly. Helping Alexandre was the right thing to do.

"Does she get visitors?" asked Jean de Dieu.

"No. Since Alexandre's been gone, I haven't seen anyone. We're the only people she sees. Her pension cheque comes in the mail. Nadège goes with her to the bank to cash it."

Suzy was idly stroking the sleeping child's head. "I'd be glad to go to her place. I know you're all taking a lot of risks for me. I'll try to keep Rodolfo from making noise. He's usually very calm. It's the change in environment that upsets him."

Hans, sitting on the arm of the couch, cleared his throat. "How long before she leaves?" he asked Jean de Dieu without a trace of an accent. No one knew how he managed to conceal his origins so well. A hidden talent.

"I had planned seventy-two hours. But what Armando says is forcing me to act faster. Forty-eight hours."

Armando gave a sigh of relief.

Jean de Dieu kept his voice low. "Suzy and Rodolfo will leave with me. I can't give you details. All I can say is that the destination is Lisbon. I have to finalize the plans with Hans. Prince Antonio has been informed, of course."

Nadège asked, "So, if it's soon, she can wait here, can't she?"

Armando turned to Jean de Dieu for his opinion.

"No, we have to avoid any possibility of someone informing. Suzy will stay at Madeleine's place tonight. The old woman must already be asleep. Do you think you can take her there, Nadège?"

"Yes, Madeleine doesn't ask questions. She's sweet and passive. She loves children. All she wants to do is wait for her son to come back."

The meeting didn't go on much longer after that. Jean de Dieu asked Hans to leave first. He spoke to Suzy. "Don't worry. Everything will be fine at Madeleine's."

Ten minutes after Hans had slipped outside like a cat in the night, Jean de Dieu followed.

When Nadège brought Suzy to Madeleine's place, the old woman was sleeping like a log. The child, in his mother's arms, didn't bat an eye. Nadège had brought the small suitcase containing Suzy's few possessions and things for the child. There was no longer any sign that they had been at Armando's.

In their bed, Armando and Nadège held each other tight. They felt guilty for relocating Suzy to Madeleine's. Nadège shed a few tears. She didn't need to explain herself to her husband. He had a lump in his throat himself. They would never forgive themselves if something bad happened to little Rodolfo. They had been trying to have a baby for a long time. Rodolfo's presence in their apartment had rekindled their desire to be parents. But they knew that bringing a child into the world in wartime was not a good idea.

Prince Antonio and the Firebird

The Angolan prince was stirring his coffee in the cafeteria of the Alverca military air base some thirty minutes from Lisbon. Across from him sat Captain Tiago Esteves, better known as *o pássaro de fogo*, the Firebird. He was a legendary pilot. A hero of the Viriatos Legion, the Portuguese volunteers who had fought in the Spanish Foreign Legion beside the Nationalists in the Spanish Civil War. He had distinguished himself in General Franco's army by bombing columns of Republicans, piloting a fighter plane called the Gloster Gladiator. It was a very flexible bird, a biplane with a front propeller. His nickname, the Firebird, came from the way he strafed the enemy at low altitude, with the victims able to see the fire spitting from the guns. An ace of aerial acrobatics, he had rejoined the Portuguese army after the war. But despite all his medals and honours, Tiago Esteves missed combat. His country's neutrality led him to seek action wherever he could find it.

A friend of a friend had put Prince Antonio in contact with the pilot. The prince made his proposal: a flight from the air base to the Bourges Airport, not far from Paris.

The pilot looked at him, intrigued. Did he have official authorization from Portugal and the Germans?

The prince reached into the inner pocket of his blue coat and took out the authorization the lawyer Senhor Santiago Miranda had given him that morning, signed by Salazar. The pilot carefully read the document, which contained the terms "secret mission" and "valuable package." An official representative of the German government had also signed it, guaranteeing receipt of the "valuable package."

"How much are you paying?" the pilot asked, a cigarette dangling from the left corner of his mouth.

The prince said he would pay several hundred dollars, adding that the money was coming from the coffers of the Portuguese government. Tiago raised his eyebrows, impressed.

It was the prince's turn to ask a question. Was it possible to get a civilian aircraft with several seats?

The pilot flicked the ash from his cigarette into an ashtray on the table. "Yes, it's possible." He was thinking of the Caudron C.440 Goéland, a twin-engine low-wing monoplane. It was a French-made aircraft developed in the mid-thirties. The main landing gear retracted into the engine nacelles. The cabin could hold six passengers, and there were baggage compartments and a toilet. The bird was sitting in one of the hangars of a flying club not far from the air base. It was a civilian aircraft, but it was a tough plane that had always impressed the Portuguese pilot. The French knew how to build good airplanes, he reflected. "One way or round trip?"

"Round trip."

"And the date?"

"I don't know exactly. But soon. You'll have to be ready to leave on short notice."

The pilot smiled, playing absent-mindedly with his moustache. "You civilians have no idea what it takes to fly a plane. You have to make a flight plan, choose a good route that avoids enemy aircraft, and check the weather forecast. I need to know at least a week in advance."

"No. Three days in advance."

The prince's commanding tone surprised the pilot. He was so accustomed to being admired that he wondered if the man knew he was talking to a military hero. But the money was enticing. He named his price. It had gone up to one thousand dollars. He explained that borrowing the Goéland wouldn't be cheap.

"Agreed," answered the prince without batting an eye. He wasn't going to quibble over the cost. It wasn't his money.

They set a date for their next meeting. Not on a military base. In Lisbon. The prince invited him to a pleasant restaurant in his neighbourhood. On his own turf. The pilot accepted, fascinated by this elegant African who didn't seem to know him, the Firebird. "Do you know who I am?" he finally asked as they shook hands.

"*O pássaro de fogo*."

The Portuguese pilot smiled, satisfied.

The African kept hold of his hand. "And you know who I am?"

The pilot answered, "Prince Antonio."

"I'm the man no one puts anything over on." These words were accompanied by a firm handshake.

"So we understand each other," concluded Tiago solemnly.

The General Calls Major Baumeister on the Carpet

General Erich von Bose did not contact his major immediately after he learned about the compromising photos. He let a few days go by. Neither the Pétainist newspapers nor the Resistance publications seemed to have been informed of Major Baumeister's misadventures. So his superior was in no hurry to discuss the matter with him. In addition, a public scandal would have tarnished his name as well. Among other things, he was responsible for the Wehrmacht's image in Paris.

The major entered von Bose's office for their regular weekly meeting, not suspecting that the general was aware of his latest indiscretion. The purpose of these meetings was to do a review of the resisters who had talked under torture and the wretches who had taken their secrets to the grave. Von Bose didn't care about the loss of the prisoners' lives in the hands of the major and his team. Only the results mattered to him. He wanted them to talk before they died. Otherwise, the enemy remained in control of the situation.

The general always saw Baumeister last, after the other officers assigned to interrogations. The major didn't always express himself clearly and his superior wanted to have time to get the information out of him. It was as if that boorish, conniving man was fighting his own war, seeking his own personal victory. For example, the major's secretary never transcribed the confessions. The major decided what was important and he personally typed what the prisoners said. Also, all too often lately, his suspects seemed to be slipping through his fingers. Von Bose thought of the Angolan prince who was trafficking in diamonds. That Black must be working for the Portuguese PVDE. He had managed to go back to Lisbon before they could question him. A lost opportunity to turn him into a double agent. There had also been the murder of a major black market alcohol dealer, Simon Giraudoux, alias Pastis. Von Bose had been counting on him to infiltrate the group of bourgeois Parisians that was financing the Resistance. The man had been murdered in his apartment in the 16th arrondissement despite surveillance by the major's men. Things were getting out of hand.

After the mandatory salute, Baumeister opened a file folder. He was about to read out the list of torture victims who had confessed that week when von Bose interrupted him. "You'll give my secretary the report. I want you to tell me about the owner of Chez Pierrette." His tone seemed almost courteous.

Baumeister wondered if the general was in a particularly good mood. "It was a false lead. I had to let her go. There was nothing to be had from her," he replied.

He wanted to take another look in the file folder on his lap, but his superior insisted. "No, Major Baumeister, I don't want the report today. Explain why Pierrette was freed."

The general's insistence was a red flag for the major. Von Bose knew something. Baumeister put the file folder down, cleared his throat discreetly, and asked, "Was it Lieutenant Betz who informed you?"

"No. I don't have to disclose the name of my informant to you. But Lieutenant Betz had nothing to do with it, and if I hear that you blame him, it will be a demotion for you. Is that clear?"

"Yes, General," Baumeister conceded, with a cold stare.

"I received this." Von Bose laid the compromising photo Betz had given him on the desk. "Are there others?" he inquired.

The major, humiliated, took a deep breath. "I received three others."

Erich von Bose knew that. He had heard it straight from Betz. However, he wanted to make sure Baumeister wasn't going to lie. "What did you do with them?"

"They've been destroyed."

"Very well."

The major went to grab the photo off the desk.

"No. Leave it there." The general got to his feet and picked the photo up again to look at it in front of his officer, whose face was crimson. "What have you done to track down the blackmailer?"

Baumeister fidgeted, unable to sit still in his chair. He admitted he didn't have any clues. He mentioned the fake mailman who had delivered the letter and the falsified date on the envelope. A bold job, impeccable work.

"And your mistress? Don't tell me you're in love?" The general uttered the words as if love was a kind of venereal disease.

"I couldn't carry out a proper interrogation in my apartment. That sly woman took advantage of my need for discretion and refused to talk."

"I see. So you're at the same point you were at when you received the photos."

The observation embarrassed the major even more. He was mortified. He ventured a question that had been running through his mind. "Was I wrong to let Pierrette go?"

"No. It was a tactical retreat. In addition, it must please her cousin the commissioner and his colleagues. It let them think they've won." He looked at the photo again and Baumeister felt the knife being twisted in the wound. "It's an 'Aunt Minnie,'" von Bose commented.

"As I said, the work of an expert," Baumeister replied. "I suspect resistance members from Eastern Europe. Poles, Bulgarians, they have the expertise."

"No, they would have plastered them all over Paris. If they haven't, you can assume there aren't many of them, and that it's a question of personal rather than collective revenge. Do you have any idea who would want to take revenge on you?"

"The list is long," admitted the major.

"I know. Our work inevitably gives rise to deep resentments." The general peered at the photo, drumming his fingers on the desk. He was doing it deliberately to deflate the major's ego, to humiliate him to the point where he would do anything asked of him, like a lapdog. "I almost sent a report to Berlin. And then I changed my mind. Your performance, even with all its ups and downs, is appreciated. But your work methods are somewhat questionable. For example, I have the impression that the information you've extracted from tortured prisoners is rather fragmentary. I am your commanding officer. You have to tell me everything."

The major lowered his eyes and kept a diplomatic smile on his face. He had been sent to Paris by a general who was higher in rank than this von Bose. He wasn't intimidated. Von Bose's tactics would have worked with the other officers. But Baumeister, even with his self-esteem in tatters, intended to maintain a certain independence. "My information is as complete as possible. In certain circumstances, the prisoners reveal information that bears no relation to the reasons for which they were arrested. In such cases, I have to assess my findings. Sorry that they sometimes seem 'fragmentary.'"

His superior stared at him with his steely blue eyes. "I am giving you authorization to interrogate your mistress."

"In the basement?"

"Yes, but after nightfall. Put a hood on her. No one must know who she is. Do whatever you want with her. She must talk. Since the blackmailer hasn't given your photos to the newspapers, he probably won't do it. But we have to apprehend him before he changes his mind." He sat down again, still holding the photo. He made as if to hand it over but then snatched it away. In fact, he had no intention of returning it, a tactic the major recognized. "I'll keep it in a safe place as evidence," the general said. "It will be useful to you when you interrogate your mistress."

The major didn't answer. He stood up quickly and gave a formal salute.

Just as Baumeister opened the door to leave, the general said, "Instead of screwing around, why don't you just get yourself a pet."

The comment made Baumeister frown. But the general could only see the back of his head and he returned to his work. The secretary wished the major a good day, but he didn't answer. She observed that his face was red with anger and his gait was martial.

Baumeister went directly to his office without saying a word to anyone along the way. He locked the door behind him and telephoned Angèle. Her phone rang, but there was no answer. He hung up, still furious. He opened the bottom drawer of his desk and took out a glass and a bottle of Scotch. He took a good slug. That calmed his rage. He decided to go and see Angèle that very evening. He would set a trap for her. He would have some fun during the interrogation. All things come to those who wait.

The Police Visit Nadège and Armando

Suzy and her son had been at Madeleine's for barely twenty-four hours when police officers knocked loudly on Armando and Nadège's door. Two serious-looking men in grey winter coats entered as soon as the door was opened. The couple was eating their evening meal. It was a turnip and sardine soup, with garlic bread. Nadège had been about to take some to Suzy in the other apartment. She greeted the policemen with a smile.

"Judicial police. We were informed that there are foreigners living under your roof."

Armando almost choked on his soup. He coughed.

Nadège came to his rescue. "Certainly not, Monsieur. It's just the two of us living here."

Her husband looked shocked and added, "You can search the apartment. There's only us."

Accompanied by Armando, the policemen checked every room. They searched the closets and under the beds. The bedroom where Suzy and her child had slept had no sheets on the bed.

Then they asked the couple for their papers. "It's routine, we have to verify who you are. You have a foreign accent, Monsieur. Where are you from?"

"From Brazil. I'm a musician," answered Armando, showing them a photo of himself in the living room, guitar in hand.

The thinner of the two police officers glanced at it quickly without smiling.

The fatter one read, "Armando Luis Pereira," and asked, "Are you the owner of the café Le Croissant Doré?"

"Yes, that's me. You're welcome there whenever you want to come, Messieurs. I'll make you a Brazilian coffee, on the house."

The thinner one looked suspicious. "The tenant upstairs said she heard a baby crying in the past few days. You don't have a child. What was that?"

Nadège was shocked to learn there was an informer living above her. The woman had a pleasant voice and such a gentle manner. A teacher in a neighbourhood high school. She had an unemployed husband and two school-age children.

Armando laughed, looking at Nadège, who was trying to smile. "It was her cousin's child! Her cousin Isabelle from Brittany. She stayed with us for a few days. Her son Marcel had colic and he cried a lot. Mystery solved."

The thin policeman didn't like the Brazilian's jaunty attitude. "Monsieur, I know that in Brazil the police are something of a joke! But here, we don't make fun of law enforcement officers. I can lock you up whenever I want. So let's be serious!"

"Yes, Officer," answered Armando solemnly.

Nadège, who had been observing the two policemen, noted that the fat one didn't like it when his partner yelled. "I made rhubarb pudding for dessert," she said. "Would you like to taste it?" She looked at the fat one, smiling politely.

The policemen exchanged surprised looks. Not only was the Brazilian not taking them seriously, but his wife was talking about dessert. The thin one took a deep breath and rolled his eyes. Just when he was about to tell them off, the fat one said, "Yes, I'd love to taste it."

His partner stared at him with angry eyes.

"You can taste it too," the fat one said to him.

This comment threw the thin one off. He lost his indignant look. Armando and Nadège realized then that he wasn't really angry, he just wanted to make an impression. Armando rubbed his hands together and took out a bottle and two glasses. "I have a Calvados here I'd like you to taste. A gift from before the Occupation. You'll tell me what you think."

The policemen offered no objection. It was rare to find a decent bottle in wartime. It would do them good to warm their palates. A café owner always had something nice tucked away.

They were all standing around the table. The officers had to get going quickly in order to continue their search for Jews in hiding. The fat one tasted the rhubarb pudding and congratulated the cook. They both drank some Calvados. It brought a smile to the thin one's lips. "That's good stuff. Keep it safe or someone will steal it from you." He sounded friendly, and that was a good sign. "So, is that cousin back in Brittany?"

"Yes, she left a few days ago."

"Oh, okay," said the fat one. "We'll be going now."

They left without further ado, closing the door behind them. The thin one was going on about the Calvados. "Good stuff," he kept repeating. He couldn't wait to see the end of wartime restrictions. The fat one had enjoyed himself too. He was thinking of the rhubarb pudding. "Wait for me in the car. I won't be long. I need to get that recipe from her."

He climbed the stairs quickly and knocked again, more softly this time. The Brazilian opened the door, his mouth full of pudding.

"I'd like the recipe for that rhubarb pudding." said the officer. "My wife is always looking for ways to make inexpensive desserts."

Armando opened the door wide. Nadège got a piece of paper and a pencil and started to write her recipe. You had to start by boiling the rhubarb in water, and then add saccharine, sugar being a rare commodity. Just when she was writing that you had to add barley cream, the apartment door opened again. It was Suzy coming to get her turnip and sardine soup. She had been getting hungry. The little boy was in her arms.

Nadège turned around abruptly and dropped her pencil. Armando and the policeman, who were talking about how hard it was to find sugar in Paris, were suddenly silent. Suzy realized she had walked into a lion's den. Armando looked defeated.

The officer approached Suzy, who was rooted to the spot. He said in a low voice, "So you're Madame's 'cousin,' and that's the baby that was crying."

The other three were completely silent.

The policeman held out his little finger to Rodolfo, who grabbed it and smiled. "A little Black child," murmured the officer, "a cute little Black boy." He stroked the toddler's hair, marvelling at the curls. He turned back towards Nadège. "So how's that recipe coming?"

She stammered something unintelligible and started writing again. Suzy didn't dare try to leave for fear he would call her back.

Nadège handed the recipe to the policeman, who read it quickly. "Thank you." As he was leaving, he stopped in front of Armando. "I didn't see anything. There's another visit scheduled in three days to catch you unawares. Make sure your Jewess isn't here anymore. Or else she'll be picked up." He turned to Nadège again and held up the recipe. "My wife is going to be happy!"

His colleague called out to him from the bottom of the stairs," Hey! Are you coming?"

"Yes, yes. Let's go."

Suzy went back to Madeleine's apartment at the end of the hallway. There, at least, she didn't feel threatened. The old woman had accepted her presence without asking any questions. She was Nadège's friend, and her cute toddler cheered things up in the apartment. She kept telling Suzy her son was soon going to come back. It was a matter of days. Sometimes she talked to herself, to her dead husband, or to the beloved son. Her harmless delusions were better than the insanity of the Nazis, thought Suzy.

Armando had to calm his wife, who had fallen into his arms, her legs giving way under her. He'd caught her at the last minute. He offered her some of his excellent Calvados and she accepted it although she never drank. She needed something to keep from screaming in terror. The alcohol quickly took effect. She lay down on the couch in the living room with a blanket pulled up to her neck.

Armando left Nadège to take supper to Suzy. He found her with eyes red from crying. Rodolfo was playing on the floor, carefree, a rattle in his little hand. Armando put the tray of food down. "Eat while it's still hot. There's no need to worry. It's over now. You're with us, you and Rodolfo."

"But tomorrow..."

"Tomorrow, Jean de Dieu will come and get you. He keeps his promises. He and Hans will take you away far from here. You'll be joining Prince Antonio. You'll see, everything will be fine. But you have to eat to keep up your strength."

She obeyed, comforted. The Brazilian knew how to reassure people. She gave a piece of sardine to the toddler, who chewed it with relish.

"You're very lucky. He's so beautiful." Armando planted a kiss on the child's cheek and left the apartment to go check on his wife. She was sound asleep. When he saw that everything seemed to be back to normal, he knelt in front of the crucifix on the bedroom wall and prayed, his face covered in tears.

In Pursuit of Angèle

The Nazi had been sitting in his mistress's apartment for two hours. It was late at night and he remained in the dark to avoid revealing his presence. Parisians were instructed to keep their lights off to deter aerial attacks by the British, and they obeyed. Although the RAF mostly targeted the suburbs, where the factories were located, the city of Paris wasn't spared.

Baumeister had a key to the apartment. Angèle had given it to him as a sign of trust. The ticking of the living room clock was driving him crazy and the darkness was making him think dark thoughts. "When I get my hands on that woman, she'll pay for her treachery," he muttered.

Hermann, waiting downstairs, had been ordered to hide the Mercedes so that the prey would not suspect anything. The major finally turned on the light, exasperated. How dare she play hide-and-seek with him? He would move heaven and earth to apprehend her.

Another hour had passed when Hermann knocked at the door and called to the major, trying not to shout. The major opened the door and looked at him, worried.

"Angèle has left Paris. I called Lieutenant Betz. He got the passenger list of a train that crossed the border to Switzerland this morning. Her name was on it."

For the major, this news was one more insult from Angèle. He also saw it as a confession of guilt. "Okay, Hermann. Take me home. We'll contact our Swiss informants first thing tomorrow."

On the way back, Baumeister gritted his teeth to keep from screaming in rage. He didn't believe the Swiss informants would be of any help. They never revealed anything. He had told Hermann that just to save face. He had already worked with the Swiss authorities to try to locate fugitives. Those people dragged their feet, in keeping with the country's neutrality. To the major, Switzerland was the land of vain hopes, of actions that were promised but never carried out. Of the ten fugitives he had asked them for in recent months, not one had been turned over to him. They were all suspects who had crossed the border with their real passports, as Angèle Gross had. He wasn't even counting those who had crossed under assumed names. Angèle, a suspect in a case of morals and blackmail, would get a new identity and vanish just like the others; he didn't expect the Swiss police to capture and extradite her. They had other arrests to make. He had missed an opportunity for revenge when she had come to his apartment. He pounded his fist on the soft seat of his Mercedes in frustration. Angèle had won, and she deserved to be flayed alive for her betrayal. Grimacing with rage, powerless to do anything, Baumeister met his driver's worried gaze in the rear-view mirror and tried to appear calm.

Once home, he poured himself a stiff shot of American whisky. All he wanted was some good news. He had the impression that his failures had begun with the prince from Angola who had evaded him and disappeared to Lisbon. What if that strange character was the source of all his misfortunes? Had he underestimated those Blacks? The translator with his polished French seemed to have vanished into thin air. The prince's driver too. He wasn't going to the jazz clubs anymore. And now Angèle had taken a powder. Who had tipped them off? No answer to that question. Fortunately, his men held the record in his department for the highest number of Jews arrested. Otherwise, von Bose would already have put him on a train to Russia.

The Gare de Lyon,
a Train for Guerche-sur-l'Aubois

Jean de Dieu was to take Suzy and her little boy to the Free Zone, which was controlled by Pétain's Vichy government. Then they would board another train, to Marseille. The prince had given them the address of a Portuguese couple there, on Rue des Catalans, with whom Suzy and the child would spend the night. Franco Rocha was a former governor of Angola who ran an import-export company. The following day, Suzy and the child would board a ship sailing under the flag of Brazil, the Yemanjá, named after an Afro-Brazilian goddess. The ship would stop at Lisbon before continuing on to the port of Santos, in the state of São Paulo in Brazil.

Sitting in the waiting room of the Gare de Lyon, Jenny was using her mirror again. Her role was to make sure the couple and the child were not being watched. Jean de Dieu and Suzy were waiting for the boarding announcement with the toddler on Suzy's lap. Except for the scowls of some of the older men and women who didn't approve of interracial marriage, the travellers in the station didn't seem to be paying much attention to them. Jenny was seated not far from the couple, and she was wearing a stylish coat and a hat with a hatpin. She put away her little mirror and started leafing through a women's magazine. Jean de Dieu had given her simple instructions. If she detected imminent danger, she was to get up and leave the magazine on her seat. If everything was fine, she was to remain there until boarding time.

Hans was a little farther away. He had dressed with special care. He was sporting a new wool coat, a white fedora, a beige striped suit, and polished black and white oxfords, and there was a case containing a saxophone at his feet. He too was waiting to board. He was playing the role of a Caribbean musician in order to draw attention to himself.

This wasn't difficult for him, since he had many friends who were musicians. The diversionary tactic had been Jean de Dieu's idea, and it was effective. The security men had already asked for his papers twice. Jean de Dieu had insisted that Hans travel without his pistol because of the likelihood of searches, and Hans had agreed to leave it at home. But Jean de Dieu wondered if his friend had a weapon hidden in the saxophone case.

At boarding time, Jenny smiled goodbye to Jean de Dieu. Carrying a suitcase, he boarded the train in first class with Suzy and the child. Hans also got on the train. He sat three rows away from them. They were surrounded by German officers, who were taking little interest in them. The Germans were talking among themselves, ignoring the people they had defeated. They were going back to their postings not far from the Free Zone. The atmosphere among them felt almost pleasant to Jean de Dieu. The other passengers were preoccupied with survival amid the uncertainties of life in wartime, such as the possibility of an aerial attack on the railway.

Suzy didn't say anything, she was looking after the child. She had given him milk before the departure and he was dozing, snuggled happily against her. There were several stops, and Jean de Dieu squeezed Suzy's hand at each one to tell her not to worry. Hans exchanged a few remarks with his seatmate, a Frenchman. But the man's lack of knowledge of music made the discussion short. That suited Hans, since he needed to avoid unnecessary conversation.

The train slowed down in the department of Nièvre. There was a checkpoint not far from the town of Nevers. Jean de Dieu looked out the window. German soldiers armed to the teeth surrounded the train. An officer, speaking mangled French in a commanding voice, ordered all the passengers to get off. Jean de Dieu whispered to Suzy not to speak unless she was spoken to. They had gone through a check by the French police at a stop two hours earlier, and she had risen to the occasion. He hoped the same would be the case with the Germans. Jean de Dieu knew Hans would react at the least sign of trouble.

João de Deus Kassoma was wanted by the Gestapo. According to the report Major Baumeister had distributed in the occupied zone, he was suspected of involvement in the murder of an informer known as Pastis. Baumeister had also circulated a composite sketch of Suzy Lazowski, a foreign Jewess who was on the run. Because of that, Jenny had spent the evening before their departure dying Suzy's hair and changing her hairstyle. They hoped she would have less chance of getting caught as a brunette.

They stood in line in the cold on the Nevers station platform. From time to time, the Wehrmacht would take a passenger away. The poor soul would try in vain to convince the Nazi officer behind his table that they had the wrong person. The soldiers would lead the prisoner away to certain death. The dogs, German shepherds, were barking excitedly, and little Rodolfo started to cry. The line was moving forward, slowly. The suspense was nerve-wracking.

Suzy finally arrived in front of the interrogator, the child clinging to her chest.

"*Papiere!*"

She took her documents out. Her name was Lara Camara, and she was the wife of Martin Camara, who was from Portuguese Guinea. That had been Prince Antonio's idea. He knew no one would know anything about the obscure Portuguese colony in Africa. That made Martin Camara neutral and insignificant. The colony provided Portugal with vegetable oil and other agricultural products.

Lara Camara's maiden name was Degroote and she was born in Belgium. Jean de Dieu, who knew the Belgians well, gave Suzy a few expressions from the country to boost her confidence. Being Flemish, Lara Degroote didn't belong to the francophone community. That would explain the woman's broken French.

The soldier asked her if she was travelling alone and she answered, with an accent she hoped would sound Belgian, that her husband was behind her. The soldier motioned to Jean de Dieu to hand him his papers. With a polite smile, Jean de Dieu complied. The baby's name was included on the mother's document. Of course, the papers were forgeries. The inspector asked their destination and Jean de Dieu said they were going to Marseille and then to Portuguese Guinea so that his parents could meet the child.

The officer shook his head. He didn't believe them. "I think you're trying to get away to the United States." He poked his colleague with his elbow. "What do you think?"

But his colleague was eyeing Hans and not paying attention to the conversation.

"They say they're going to Marseille and then to a place called Guinea or something?"

"Portuguese Guinea," repeated Jean de Dieu in a friendly tone of voice.

The soldier behind his table asked his distracted colleague in German, "Have you ever heard of that hole?"

"Let them go," the colleague answered in German. "They'll be stuck in Marseille for months. There aren't many passenger ships to Africa. We'll have plenty of time to check if they're fugitives and pick them up there if necessary."

The soldier in charge didn't seem convinced. He looked closely at the couple's papers. But the sound of ferocious barking broke his concentration. A passenger, who couldn't take waiting in line any longer had run towards the woods nearby. A dog had caught him and was mauling him on the ground. "Okay," the soldier conceded. "A couple with a child is easy to find."

Hans lowered his head to hide the fact that he had understood those words. He waited his turn, knowing that the soldiers were going to search him methodically. Once again, Jean de Dieu's strategy worked like a charm. The soldiers let the couple pass and concentrated on Hans. "French, eh?"

"Yes, Caribbean. From Guadeloupe."

Jean de Dieu wasn't worried about Hans's papers. The passport was a good fake. The forger guaranteed his products.

The officer standing beside the soldier bent down to read the document at the same time as his colleague. He was a captain with an icy stare and a square jaw. "Follow me," he said to Hans in perfect French.

They stepped away from the line.

"Richard Alexis. You're a musician?"

"Yes, a jazz musician. I play saxophone," he added, pointing at the case on the ground.

The captain asked him to raise his arms and patted him down from head to toe without saying a word. The other passengers were glancing over, curious about how this scenario would play out.

The captain continued, a nasty smile on his lips, "I'm quite familiar with the clubs in Paris. Where have you performed?"

Without raising an eyebrow, Hans listed three jazz clubs in the city.

The captain nodded at a soldier who had a dog on a leash. The soldier ordered the animal to sniff the case.

"Are you going to play in Marseille?"

Hans gave him the name of the club where he was going to play that very evening.

"Open the case."

Hans looked surprised and unlatched the case. The dog growled and the other dogs joined in. The open case contained only the instrument.

"I've never heard of Richard Alexis. Coleman Hawkins, yes. Lester Young too. And Lester Young is one hell of a pianist. Don't you think?"

Hans frowned. "You're mistaken. Lester Young plays tenor saxophone."

The captain saw that he wasn't going to catch him out so easily. He decided to give him back his papers. But Hans knew the Nazi wasn't finished with him. He could see in his eyes that he still intended to trip him up.

Jean de Dieu was watching this back-and-forth out of the corner of his eye. They were waiting for the order to reboard the train.

"Where are your things?"

"In the baggage car."

"Nothing to report inside? You musicians love to party. Maybe there's booze or drugs." He ordered Hans to go get his suitcase.

Meanwhile, the passengers were being allowed back on the train. Boarding took about ten minutes, and the captain continued questioning Hans. He asked him for his address in Paris and for the names of musicians he had played with, and he wrote everything down. A soldier opened his suitcase, which contained clothes and personal effects. The captain searched it disdainfully with his gloved hands. He scattered the contents on the ground, but found nothing compromising. He asked his lieutenant in a loud voice, "When is the next train coming?"

"In about ten minutes," answered the lieutenant. "Do you want to keep him here? Blacks talk better with a pistol at their temple."

The captain smiled, but shook his head. "No, we have to let this train go. Or else we'll have the major on our backs." He shrugged and continued in German, "He's an ugly bugger, isn't he?"

"Yes. We should hold him."

The captain took out the saxophone. After checking the inside of the case to see if there was a false bottom, he said in German in a haughty tone of voice, "You look like those bastards we had in Germany."

Hans looked at him, expressionless, "Sorry, I don't understand."

The man went back to French. "You're mulatto, aren't you?"

"I'm Guadeloupian," answered Hans calmly.

"Okay, Mister Jazzman." the captain said in English. "Play it for me."

Hans looked at him without reacting.

"Do you understand?" he shouted in French. "Play your instrument. If it's yours."

"Right here? Now?" Hans asked.

"Hurry up," said the captain, his hand on his automatic pistol. "We don't have a lot of time. There's another train coming. I'm warning you, if you don't know how to play, I'll shoot you right here." He spat out the words with a grimace of disgust.

Watching from the train window, Jean de Dieu saw his friend pick up the instrument and understood immediately what he was being asked to do. "My God," he muttered. His throat tightened. He regretted ordering Hans to travel unarmed. It would be better if he died fighting than if he was killed without being able to defend himself. Suzy also saw the whole scene. She knew that if Hans was killed, her escape would be compromised. Jean de Dieu would surely have trouble carrying out his mission without his brother-in-arms. Her fate and that of her child depended on them.

Hans put his lips to the mouthpiece of the saxophone and closed his eyes. George Gershwin's "Summertime" resounded in the Nevers station, echoing off the walls, mesmerizing everyone. Even the dogs were motionless.

Realizing he had made an error, the captain ordered Hans to stop before he got to the second verse.

Jean de Dieu turned his head towards his friend in disbelief. Hans played the saxophone beautifully. He felt like running over and hugging him, but he just squeezed Suzy's hand and exchanged a quiet smile with her.

The Nazi turned on his heel, furious. Hans hurriedly repacked his scattered clothes. There was no time to lose because the train was starting to move. The soldiers remained in place with their dogs. They were waiting for other passengers to terrorize.

A Singer in Lisbon

Prince Antonio was waiting for the Firebird in a restaurant in the Alfama district. The place was called *O Garfo Mágico*, the magic fork. It was a damp winter evening, the icy rain had just stopped and the cobblestones glistened in the twilight. The prince had walked through the maze of narrow streets in his neighbourhood to immerse himself in the atmosphere of this city that he loved so much. He didn't notice anyone who looked suspicious, like the shady character he had encountered the last time.

Sitting with his back to an ochre wall, he was listening to a corpulent black singer who was accompanying herself on the accordion. She must have been about fifty, and her fingers with their blue nail polish moved effortlessly over the keys of the instrument. She was wearing a red dress that was snug at the hips, and black high-heeled shoes. Her words, in a Portuguese creole, spoke of leaving and lost love. The prince was enjoying this melancholy music, which was called *saudade*, while sipping a glass of white wine. The singer walked among the tables, her gaze soft and sultry. She had several necklaces of costume jewelry resting on her generous bosom. Prince Antonio didn't know her name, but he had previously seen her perform in another restaurant. He took out a banknote and placed it on the table for her. She continued playing with one hand, and with the other, tucked the money into her dress. She thanked him with a big smile.

The pilot, Tiago Esteves, entered the restaurant and stopped for a moment to let the singer pass through the narrow space between the tables. "I see you're a music lover," he said to the prince after the customary greetings.

"It all depends on what music I'm listening to."

Esteves raised an eyebrow. He decided not to say anything more about the subject. He asked the prince what wine he was drinking. The prince told him, and the pilot ordered the same.

The two men talked about the tense atmosphere in Lisbon in recent years. The pilot found the influx of refugees and the surveillance measures of the Salazar government depressing. He confided that even he, a hero of the Spanish war, a fervent believer in the New State, was under surveillance. "The PVDE is on my heels. Why? I don't know. I support this regime. Did you know that the political police report directly to Salazar? Not to the Minister of the Interior."

The Angolan prince had to be careful when talking about Portuguese politics. He had been able to obtain an entry visa for Suzy and her son from the Portuguese legation in Vichy thanks to Santiago Miranda. He wasn't going to antagonize the only country that was helping him. "No, I wasn't aware."

The pilot realized that the prince wasn't going to engage in criticism of the regime.

They ordered their dinner. The prince chose a *Francesinha*, literally "a little French girl," a kind of croque-monsieur made with cheese and chicken. It was accompanied by fried potatoes. Tiago Esteves chose cod with a corn bread crust.

"Do you have the money?" he asked the prince.

The prince showed him the leather briefcase under the table. "With the compliments of the Salazar government."

The irony was not lost on the pilot, who laughed out loud. The restaurant had become quiet again after the performance by the singer.

The sparse clientele made it easy for the prince to check his surroundings. "So, in three days the airplane will be ready, right?" he asked, and waited solemnly for the reply.

"Yes, everything will be ready. Can I know what the 'package' is that we'll be taking to Paris?"

"It would be premature to tell you. You'll see when we board the plane."

When it was time for dessert, the pilot apologized. "I'll have to leave now if I want to find a taxi quickly. It's getting late, and walking in Lisbon with all this money isn't advisable."

"You did come prepared, all the same." Prince Antonio had immediately noticed the lump in the inner pocket of the pilot's dark suit.

"You're very perceptive," said Esteves. "I never go out without my weapon. If one of those anti-Francoists running around the city tried to get me, I'd give him a warm welcome."

"You're not the only one who's armed," said the prince, who was carrying his ivory-headed cane with the blade in it. He wanted to assert his authority over the pilot. War hero or not, Esteves was working for him. "Count the money."

"Here?"

"Yes, open the briefcase and count it."

Hearing the prince's commanding tone, the pilot decided to comply. Something told him he shouldn't rub the man the wrong way. A Black prince who was getting funds from the Salazar government for a secret mission was to be taken seriously. He gave the money a quick look without taking it out, did a few calculations under his breath, and closed the briefcase, satisfied. He was about to call the waiter for the bill, but the prince motioned that it wasn't necessary. Esteves shook the prince's hand by way of thanks and repeated that he would be waiting at the airfield in three days.

Prince Antonio drank a digestif and again scanned the few clients in the restaurant to check that no one was spying on him. He put his hat on and decided to walk home.

He had only taken a few steps in the street when, at a turn in the maze of streets, he heard a voice from the shadows behind him. "Your Majesty, may I have a minute of your time?"

Prince Antonio peered into the darkness. "Who is it?" His voice, steeped in authority, pierced the silence of the night. He wasn't afraid. His cane in his hand, he was ready to pull out the blade and use it if necessary.

"Your Majesty, it's only me."

He recognized the Black singer in her red dress. “What do you want?”

“There’s a man who’s looking for you.”

The prince motioned the woman to approach. She took a few steps forward and glanced behind her, worried. “I can’t stay long. I have to sing in a restaurant three blocks from here and I don’t want to be late.”

He kept his hand on his cane and gave a skeptical smile. “Have you been waiting long for me? What if I hadn’t come out?”

“I would have gone in and given you a note. But you’re here now.”

“How much do you want for telling me the name of the man who’s looking for me?”

“Nothing, Prince Antonio. Everyone in the restaurants of Alfama knows and respects you. Besides, you’re from Africa, like me.”

“São Tomé and Príncipe?” asked the prince.

The singer looked at him admiringly. “Yes. You know it?”

“No, but I studied with a young man who has the same accent as you.”

She lowered her eyes and a sad look passed over her face. “I plan to return there one day after this damn war is over, God willing.”

The prince made no comment, still on the alert.

“He’s a white man, tall and blond. Maybe forty years old. He’s not as well dressed as you. Grey coat, grey hat. A German accent, although he tries to hide it. The idiot gave me money to let him know if I saw you.”

“Does the idiot have a name?”

“Peter.”

“A phone number?”

“No. He didn’t give me one. He often comes in the evening.”

“When did you last see him?”

“Barely an hour ago.”

The prince waited for more. The singer pointed to a little restaurant on Rua de Santiago. “Don’t go there, Your Majesty. I came to warn you. I can see that the man is dangerous.”

The prince smiled again. “What’s your name?”

"Adelina Pereira Santos. But here I'm known as 'Paulina a Negra.'" She saw him reach into his inner pocket, and gestured to indicate that she didn't want money.

He took out a card with his name and phone number. "If you're ever in trouble, contact me. I'll help you."

Adelina barely had time to thank him before he headed down Rua de Santiago.

It didn't take Prince Antonio long to get to the restaurant. He wanted to confront the man who was looking for him. If the man was a killer, he was counting on his skill with the blade to take care of him before he had time to react. Before the war, he had never been without his semi-automatic pistol, a 9 mm Browning Hi-Power. He prized that model, which was made for the army. However, the presence of the Wehrmacht had forced him to avoid carrying a gun in Paris. The many checkpoints and frequent random searches had made him change his habits. He often wondered how Jean de Dieu and Hans managed to slip through the net.

Although he sometimes took his gun with him in Lisbon, it was still relatively safe there. He preferred to rely on his knife skills. As an African prince, he had learned to handle bladed weapons at a very young age. Back home, a member of the nobility had to be a warrior. His immediate reaction after the conversation with Adelina had been to try to find the man who was looking for him.

He didn't have a chance to enter the restaurant before a tall man in a grey coat and grey hat stepped out the door. His eyes met the man's cold stare.

"Ah, Prince Antonio, I presume," said the stranger in Portuguese.

The prince faced him, standing in front of the restaurant with its multicolored lanterns. "And who are you?"

"Peter Aberson. I'm a Dutch journalist. I've been looking for you for several days."

"I know."

The man eyed him and said, "Yes, so it appears. Someone must have told you. Would you like a drink?"

"No," answered the African, on his guard. "May I know why you're looking for me?"

Two men walked past them into the restaurant. That seemed to worry the mysterious Peter. "If I can't buy you a drink, let's walk together and I'll explain everything to you."

Prince Antonio noticed that the man was trying to disguise his German accent. He nodded towards an alley not far from a tram stop. There was no one there.

"I'm a journalist. According to my sources, you're wanted in Paris in connection with diamond smuggling. I wanted to meet you and get your version of the facts before publishing my article."

"What newspaper do you work for?"

"I'm a freelancer. I'll sell my story to the highest bidder."

The prince didn't believe the man for one minute. "I'm not wanted in Paris or anywhere else," he replied. "The proof is that I'm planning to go back there."

"When?"

"Soon."

The German continued as if it was an interview. "My readers would be interested in knowing why an African prince is being accused of smuggling diamonds."

The prince shrugged and took a cigar out of his coat pocket. "I'd be glad to explain. Do you have a light?"

The man took a lighter from his pocket. When he was lighting the cigar, the prince grabbed his hand and quickly turned it over. The man pulled his hand away, but it was too late. The prince had seen the death's head on his ring, which he had been wearing turned to the inside to hide it. The ring was awarded to officers of the SS for distinguished service by Heinrich Himmler, their superior.

"The death's head. You're from the Gestapo," said the prince.

"A pity," said the man. "Usually I take it off. But I didn't get a chance. I'd given up hope of finding you tonight."

"It doesn't matter. Your German accent already gave you away. What do you want of me?" He puffed on the cigar and waited patiently for the SS man to lay his cards on the table.

"Suzy Lazowski."

The prince panicked for an instant. He coughed and quickly regained his composure. "I don't know her."

"According to our colleagues in Paris, Suzy Lazowski is the mother of your son."

"Even if that were true, I don't know why you're talking to me about her."

"We've arrested her."

The prince took a deep breath. He didn't want to believe it. He knew she was no longer in Paris. If what this man was saying was true, Jean de Dieu and Hans must be dead. "I don't know her. I'm not surprised by your methods. But you're on the wrong track."

The SS man persisted. "We know you're close to the lawyer Santiago Miranda. He's a former Salazar minister. We're only asking you for information. Are they going to let the Allies establish bases in the Azores? You must know how strategic those Portuguese islands are for the war. Their location is crucial for control of the Atlantic. Have the Portuguese signed a pact with Churchill?"

Prince Antonio's heart was pounding. Was the Gestapo trying to trick him into becoming an agent for them? He took a puff on his cigar and exhaled grey smoke from his nostrils. The cold night dissipated it quickly. "This Suzy person I don't know, you're holding her in Fresnes?"

"Yes," said the SS man solemnly. "Only you can save her. Her and your child. So can we count on you?"

The prince threw his cigar to the ground. "No, Herr SS. Suzy is not in Fresnes. My informant confirmed an hour ago that she was on a train for Marseille with a visa she obtained from the Portuguese legation in Vichy. A ship to Lisbon is waiting for her there. Your bluff didn't work."

The two men stood looking at each other in the deserted alley. The SS man realized that the prince had no intention of letting him leave after what he had told him. He reached into his pocket, but he didn't have time to pull out his Luger before the prince, with a lightning movement, pierced his heart with the blade from his cane. He opened his eyes wide and crumpled to the ground. The prince heard him breathe his last. He wiped his blade on the man's clothing and walked quickly away from the body on the cobblestones.

The prince promised himself he would thank Armando for keeping him informed. Suzy mustn't miss her ship for Lisbon, because once the Gestapo learned of their agent's death, they would intensify their search for her.

Departure for Lisbon

After picking up the visa for Lisbon at the Portuguese legation in Vichy, Jean de Dieu and Suzy continued on to Marseille. Hans took a room in a quiet hotel to wait for his friend's return. They planned to make the trip back to Paris on the same train.

The Vichy-Marseille segment went without a hitch, and Franco Rocha, the former governor of Angola, came to welcome Suzy and Jean de Dieu personally on the station platform. It was late, and when they arrived at his big apartment on Rue des Catalans, Suzy and the little boy went right to one of the guest rooms to replenish their strength for the journey by ship the next day.

Rocha insisted that Jean de Dieu dine with him and his wife. They greatly missed their children, who were all in Portugal. They spoke of the years they had spent in Angola and of the kindness of His Highness Antonio Jose Henrique Dos Santos Mbwafu of the Kingdom of Kongo. Rocha said Prince Antonio had a bright future ahead of him.

Jean de Dieu listened politely to his hosts, then excused himself to rest after the long journey. The couple gave him the bedroom at the end of the hallway so that he wouldn't be disturbed if the child woke up in the night.

The next day, Jean de Dieu joined the Rochas for breakfast. Their building was on the shore of the Bay of Marseille, and the morning light woke Suzy and the child, who came to eat with the others. The atmosphere was cheerful. One would never suspect there was a war raging. The adults watched the passenger ships in the Bay and they all marvelled at the beauty of the blue sky and the soaring seagulls.

It came time to get ready. Franco Rocha went to hail a taxi. His wife insisted on giving Suzy warm clothes for the journey and went to fetch them. Jean de Dieu was left alone with Suzy and the child. He took some papers out of his coat pocket. They had travelled in the soles of his shoes and still had a few creases in them. He gave her the ticket for the boat, which included a cabin and a meal. He added her entry visa for Lisbon, her transit visa to Madrid, and her exit visa from France. The last two visas were forgeries, but of good quality. The Spanish customs agents were not very zealous when people were passing through their country. It was when people were staying that they were much more vigilant. Suzy took the documents and thanked him. He replied that it was above all due to her own courage that she had gotten to Marseille.

When Rocha came back to say that a taxi was waiting downstairs, Suzy left Rodolfo with Jean de Dieu and went to close her suitcase. The child was used to Jean de Dieu and sat in his lap playing with his favourite rattle. Rocha sat down next to Jean de Dieu. "It's important that she not miss that boat. The city is swarming with spies working for the Nazis. They have files on a lot of Jews and they've got them under surveillance. They're only allowing a trickle of them to leave. The Bompard and Terminus hotels here in Marseille are full of women and children who've been detained. They're not allowed to move around freely." His solemn tone contrasted with the cheerful mood he had displayed at breakfast. It was the first glimpse Jean de Dieu had of how anxious that warm, affable man was.

"She'll leave with the boy," was all he said in reply.

"Are you sure all the documents are in order?"

"Don't worry about anything. Thank you for your hospitality."

The answer seemed to satisfy Rocha, and he gulped down his coffee. There was something in Jean de Dieu that inspired confidence. He shared the prince's elegance and his unshakeable assurance.

The port of Marseille was teeming with people. There were boats unloading merchandise, some from Latin America, others from North Africa. Longshoremen were loading huge burlap bags onto trucks waiting to carry goods throughout Vichy France. Many of the fruits and vegetables would end up on the black market, where their prices would double.

Jean de Dieu got out of the taxi first and surveyed the surroundings before motioning to Suzy to follow with the child. The boat that was to take them to Lisbon was docked at the quayside. The Yemanjá, a commercial steamship, had three masts and a huge smokestack in the centre that belched black smoke into the blue sky. It was already allowing passengers to board.

The taxi driver, an Asian man, took the suitcase out of the trunk of his vehicle and refused Jean de Dieu's tip, saying that Franco Rocha had taken care of everything. Jean de Dieu insisted, and he finally accepted it. Porters tried to take the suitcase, but Jean de Dieu preferred to carry it himself. He motioned to Suzy to follow him and they made their way to a spot not far from the customs post. There he gave her his final instructions. "You'll speak only English."

"Okay. But Belgians speak French."

"Not all of them. According to your papers, you're Flemish, and you're going to Lisbon to introduce your son to your parents, who live there. Your husband, a Portuguese national from the colonies, will join you later."

"Okay."

"Above all, stay in your cabin. Leave it only when necessary, and always lock your door."

The young woman nodded, a worried look on her face.

"Everything will be fine." He kissed her cheek and gave her a hug so that she would appear to be his wife. "Goodbye, Rodolfo," he said to the little boy in her arms, and planted a kiss on his forehead.

Suzy joined the line to go through French customs. Jean de Dieu didn't want to wait. He knew the place was swarming with informers and spies. With a composite sketch of him in the Gestapo's hands, he felt safer in the middle of Paris, among Black men who looked like him.

Just then he felt a tap on his shoulder. Turning around, he recognized the paunchy little man standing there. He was a professor at the Institut d'Ethnologie de Paris. What was he doing here?

"Prince Antonio? Or should I call you Kassoma?"

The African pretended he didn't recognize the man. "You're mistaken, Monsieur, I don't know you."

"Come now, I'm Professor Clotaire Vasseur," he said very softly.

Jean de Dieu distinctly remembered this pedantic intellectual, a man in his fifties. He had encountered him in the corridors of the institute when he was attending classes in Prince Antonio's place. The professor taught "genetic determinism." "I don't know you, Monsieur," he insisted. "You're making a mistake."

The professor took off his heavy dark glasses and leaned forward to get a better look. "I'm sure it's you. João de Deus Kassoma. The Gestapo is looking for you."

Jean de Dieu felt his heart racing. "I don't know what you're talking about."

The professor grabbed him by the sleeve. He looked around. "Not so fast. I'm very good with faces. You're on the run, aren't you?"

Jean de Dieu changed tactics, playing for time. "Wait a minute. Vasseur? Yes, the author of the famous *Treatise on Eugenics and Human Heredity.* I never attended your lectures. Your treatise is an insult to intelligence. What are you doing in Marseille?"

The little man flushed with anger but restrained himself. "The Gestapo has arrested many of my colleagues at the institute. They uncovered a Resistance network. I have no place to teach anymore."

"I take back my comments, Professor. Come, let's go talk somewhere less crowded. I'm sure I can help you." He put his hand on the professor's shoulder to steer him away from the customs post and Suzy.

They walked together until they found a public bench behind a high flowering hedge. Jean de Dieu acted distressed at learning of the professor's troubles. He urged him to sit down away from prying eyes and tell him more. The professor, delighted to have an attentive ear, did not hesitate.

Once he was seated, Vasseur told him what he was doing in Marseille. "I'm hungry and I have no money. I came here in hope of finding a charitable soul who could help me out financially. The person I came to see must have left in a hurry. I don't know where he is."

"This war is throwing people into the street. I understand your predicament, Professor. Even I have to be careful."

This was not what Clotaire Vasseur wanted to hear. He went on the offensive. "You're always so well dressed. Give me some money, or else I'll go to the Gestapo. They'll pay to know I've seen you here in Marseille."

Jean de Dieu looked shocked at first, and then resigned. "How much do you want?"

The professor glanced at him and then turned his gaze towards the departing ships. "Enough to get to America. I have to disappear."

Jean de Dieu knew what the man was talking about. "I saw in the newspapers that several of your ethnologist colleagues were executed at Mont-Valérien recently. Why weren't you among them?"

The professor's silence betrayed him.

"You're the one who turned them in. They didn't abolish your position at the institute. You're running away from the Resistance."

The professor sighed and scratched his unshaven cheek. "I had no choice. It was them or me." Afraid he had said too much, he added, "You're no better off. How long do you think you can evade the Gestapo? They came to the institute twice, just for you. If I tell them I've seen you, they'll scour Marseille to find you. Come on, give me money and I'll keep quiet."

"My dear friend, I'm sure we can come to an understanding. Here's what I propose." In a gesture intended to appear friendly, Jean de Dieu put his arm around Vasseur's shoulders as if he was going to whisper an amount in his ear. Thinking his blackmail attempt was successful, the professor brought his head closer. With a sudden quick movement of his right hand, Jean de Dieu stabbed the professor in the chest just below his heart with a small bread knife he had taken from Franco Rocha's kitchen that very morning. Exactly as Hans had taught him, in order to avoid too much bleeding.

Taken by surprise, the professor muttered, "You've stabbed me."

Jean de Dieu covered the handle of the knife with his gloved hand, while with his other arm he pulled the professor close as if he were a friend sharing a confidence.

The little man blanched with pain. He tried to call for help, but he wasn't able to. His lungs were filling up with blood.

"We're not in one of your books on the zoological hierarchy of races," whispered Jean de Dieu in the ear of the dying man, who had maintained that Black people were base and submissive because of their circulatory system.

Jean de Dieu looked around. The hedge hid the bench where they were sitting. Vasseur was suffocating. A thin stream of blood was trickling from his mouth. His dark glasses hid his empty stare. His body was shaking with spasms, but Jean de Dieu held him firmly as if giving him a hug.

Jean de Dieu laid the professor's body, now limp, on the bench face down so that the little knife sticking out below his heart was not visible. Vasseur looked like a tramp lying dead drunk on the park bench. The people in the port went about their activities, not suspecting that a man had just been stabbed on a bench behind the flowering hedge that beautified the area. Jean de Dieu wiped his face and neck with a handkerchief to check whether there was blood on him, but found none. He strode away and hailed a taxi. After getting in, he sighed with relief. He would be able to return to Paris.

Good News for Baumeister

The major was in General Erich von Bose's office. What his superior had just told him made him rub his hands with glee. Prince Antonio was expected in Paris in less than twenty-four hours. According to the general's information, his plane, a civilian aircraft piloted by a Portuguese officer, had just taken off after a stopover in Madrid. The general stared intently at the major. "He's bringing us a 'package.'"

"Oh! What are we talking about?"

"Does the Brigada Suprema mean anything to you?"

"Leandro Barros," answered Baumeister.

"Exactly. He's on a civilian plane headed for Bourget. A gift from Salazar to our Führer."

The major crossed his legs. "That's a smart move by Prince Antonio," he admitted.

His superior lit a cigarette and continued, "It's an exchange. He intends to return to Lisbon the same day with Father Eusébio da Silva."

"That madman who makes a show of defending the Jewish race? That priest?"

"Yes, the Portuguese clergyman who dared defy our high command."

"Clever," acknowledged Baumeister. "But anything can happen to the prince once he's in Paris, right?"

The general was not surprised by the major's bloodthirsty attitude. He was the most ruthless of his torturers. "Prince Antonio has close ties with the Salazar government. Some even say he's an agent of the PVDE. We have to get him to work for us. We can't buy him off. He already has lots of money. All we can do is blackmail him. We need a mole inside the Portuguese government."

"He's coming to get his diamonds."

"Forget the diamonds. Focus on a way to force him to work for us. I read in one of your reports that he has a child with one of his mistresses. A Jewess."

"Sarah Lazowski. She goes by the name Suzy."

"Have you found this Suzy?"

"No, not yet. The translator must have helped her get away."

"Who?"

"His translator."

"Remind me who that is."

"Prince Antonio doesn't speak French. He has a translator. A tall Black, very well dressed, like his boss. He goes by the name João de Deus Kassoma, but I'm sure it's a false name. He has no Portuguese accent."

"Ah, yes. I remember seeing that name in your reports. Another one who slipped through your fingers."

Annoyed, the major defended himself. "My men were tricked. But I'll get my revenge on Prince Antonio. We'll interrogate him and find out where Suzy is hiding."

"No! I know your methods. The Führer is determined to avoid antagonizing Salazar. Imagine if the Portuguese president learned we'd mistreated his special envoy! He might think we lack respect for him. He could sign a pact with Churchill. No, we don't touch a hair on the prince's head."

The major insisted, "I won't take him to the basement, just to my office."

"Propose to him that he become a spy for us. But do it tactfully," said von Bose. "And what about the translator? Do you have any tangible evidence that can be used to put pressure on him? For example, fingerprints in Pastis's apartment?"

"None. He was careful."

Von Bose shot him an accusing look. "You're not to touch the Angolan prince, understood?"

Baumeister bit his tongue to keep from talking back. "One of our agents was recently found stabbed in Lisbon, not far from the prince's residence. I'm convinced the prince murdered him, General."

"Any witnesses?"

"No, none."

"Was that the agent who went by the name Peter Aberson?"

"Yes. You knew him?"

The general swore. "Prince Antonio is a master strategist and a cold-blooded killer. I knew Aberson well in Poland. One of our best agents."

"I'm asking you for one hour with Prince Antonio. I promise you I won't hurt him. We'll let him go after we convince him to work for us." And, he thought to himself, after he tells me where he hides his diamonds.

The steely blue gaze became even colder. "You let him leave Paris! All this is the result of your incompetence. Instead of chasing skirts, you should have concentrated on capturing him!"

Baumeister remained silent, not showing his anger. He realized that von Bose hadn't forgotten the scandalous photo Lieutenant Betz had shown him. Since then, the major's relationship with Betz was strictly limited to administrative matters.

The general took a long drag on his cigarette and stubbed it out half finished. "I must say, for all your troubles you've been lucky with this. No photos have been leaked to the newspapers. For the time being, I have nothing to hold against you. Your position is not in danger. That said, you still need to redeem yourself. Make Prince Antonio our spy."

The implicit threat was like a slap in the face to Baumeister. He had already vowed to collar Prince Antonio. It was a question of honour. He was not going to let him go back to Lisbon. Diplomatic crisis or not. "I promise you I'll make him our spy."

General Erich von Bose declared their discussion over. Since the murder of Pastis, his respect for Baumeister had greatly diminished.

Evenings Out in Paris with Hans

Since his return to the French capital, Hans was sleeping in the daytime, in different hotels in various neighbourhoods. He was pretending to be a Caribbean musician. He would put his saxophone case down in clear view on the counter when he took a room. After that, no hotel receptionist would ask him about his occupation. He didn't spend more than a week in any establishment and he always chose hotels used by prostitutes, because the ladies of the night hated the police and they would warn him if there was any chance of a raid.

At night, he would go out and get the Renault. Now repainted black, it spent its days in his friend Matty's garage. It officially belonged to Prince Antonio, but since the prince wasn't in Paris, Hans used it to drive women from the clubs to sex parties. He was well paid for his services as a nocturnal driver. The ladies had safe-conduct passes from German officers so they could circulate freely to attend the parties. Hans, quiet as a mouse, kept his hat pulled down over his eyes so as not to attract too much attention from the gendarmes checking papers in the wee hours of the morning. He always had fake papers of the highest quality and he was able to go on his way without getting arrested.

He would sometimes go to a movie at the Louxor theatre in the 10th arrondissement while waiting for the young ladies to finish their dance numbers in their respective nightclubs. He had recently seen *White Slaves*, with the German actress Camilla Horn, which dated from 1937. It was pure anti-Soviet propaganda but was presented as an adventure movie. However, he didn't go there just for the movies. He went to warm up and to watch the newsreels shown before the features. There was always an anti-Semitic documentary, then another propaganda newsreel, and finally the movie. Together, they would give him enough time to stop feeling cold. He had observed more and more exaggeration in the news about the war on the Eastern Front. To him, that meant Hitler's troops were suffering heavy losses and having difficulty advancing towards Moscow. He interpreted all the news as the opposite of what was stated.

Other evenings, he went to hear Matty playing rhythm guitar with the Hot Club de France alongside Django Reinhardt and Alix Combelle, the saxophonist. There were a lot of underground clubs where Matty played on the Left Bank. The German command in France hadn't officially banned jazz, although the Nazis hated that Black music from America.

Some nights Hans drove the beautiful Jenny to meet German officers. When she rode with him, Hans always made sure there was a bullet in the chamber of his ivory-grip Luger, which he kept under his seat. He knew that Jean de Dieu would be heartbroken if anything happened to her. Hans was like that. He was a romantic, and he'd had a few heartbreaks he never talked about. He was waiting patiently for his next love, but he didn't know if he would live long enough to find her. That was why he often said, "Another beautiful day to stay alive."

The Polish Woman and the Politician

Santiago Miranda ordered his chauffeur to go faster. He was running late. The African prince had asked him to meet his wife at the port of Lisbon. The prince hadn't told the lawyer that he and Suzy weren't married. He had to keep up appearances, especially under a regime as conservative as that of Salazar. "Hurry up, Caetano! The ship must have docked already. She must be wondering where her prince is. Floor it! If the police stop us, I'll do the talking!"

The driver obeyed immediately. The dignitary's limousine, a black Renault Suprastella convertible made in 1939, was firing on all eight cylinders and turning the heads of passersby. The motor hummed as the car sped through roundabouts and past fire hydrants and churches, forcing pedestrians to flee to the sidewalks. Caetano honked at every obstacle in the car's path. Even the pigeons yielded to it. In that early afternoon, the streets were crowded. But Caetano took shortcuts to get to the port, where he slowed down so as not to run into the longshoremen loading merchandise.

The Yemanjá was moored and empty of passengers. The ship's crew were preparing to disembark when Santiago Miranda waved to them from the dock and asked if all the passengers had left the ship. All they could hear was the dull roar of the engines. The lawyer tried to get closer, but two customs agents emerged from the crowd and grabbed his arm to hold him back. "Civilians are not allowed to board a docked ship. Move along, Senhor."

Miranda was furious. Little was forbidden to him, given his political connections. In a threatening tone, he ordered the customs agents to let go of him. He showed them the document he used to get into Salazar's offices once a week. When the agents saw the words "Personal Advisor to His Excellency Antonio de Oliveira Salazar," they snapped to attention. Travellers and their families turned around, surprised. The lawyer acted as if it was nothing unusual. "Have the passengers all disembarked?"

"Yes, Your Excellency," answered the customs agent who had forbidden him to go aboard.

Miranda put away his document and asked if they had seen a woman passenger travelling alone with a small child waiting on the pier.

The customs agents didn't know how to answer. They couldn't confirm anything. There were a lot of mothers. Some were following their husbands, others were being followed by them.

Just then, Caetano approached, eyed suspiciously by the customs agents. "This is my chauffeur," Miranda said immediately to avoid a confrontation. "What do you want?" he asked Caetano.

"Senhor, I believe the person you're looking for is over there. There's a mother with a little Black child." He indicated the direction with a nod of his head, and Miranda saw a woman with a child in her arms. Two men were examining her papers and asking her questions. They were obviously agents of the secret police.

Fuming, the lawyer walked quickly over to Suzy and the men. He jostled someone as he passed but did not excuse himself. He knew Suzy's false name for the journey, Lara Camara. Prince Antonio had told it to him. He interrupted the older of the two men, who was about fifty and was wearing a dark suit and navy blue hat. "Senhor, here's my card."

They examined the card in silence. The younger one frowned, visibly irritated.

"Now that you know who I am, I strongly advise you to let this young woman go. Her name is Lara Camara and she is my guest."

"Senhor Miranda! Please understand us, it's just a routine check," said the older officer.

The younger one added, "Senhora Camara has been waiting several minutes for her husband, and he hasn't shown up yet."

"Senhor Camara was unable to come. I've told you, this woman is my guest."

"She's a foreigner, a Belgian," said the younger officer. He was wearing a grey suit and a black hat. "You understand that we have to carry out our checks."

Suzy turned and looked at Senhor Miranda.

Miranda smiled politely. "Her papers are in order, I trust?"

"Yes," admitted the older one.

"So you can go."

Annoyed at being dismissed, the agents didn't move.

Miranda gave a deep sigh to express his exasperation. "I'll have you know, Senhores, that I regularly dine with your boss. We went to law school together."

That made the older officer pale. "I had no intention—"

"Your intentions don't interest me. Show me your identity papers."

"Captain Silvano Coelho," the officer replied.

His colleague also felt obliged to introduce himself. "Lieutenant Guido Matos."

They showed their ID cards. Two agents of the PVDE.

"You're on the point of losing your jobs, Senhores."

"I'm sorry," the older one apologized, worried. "We didn't know."

"As I told you, this woman is under my protection. I vouch for her."

"Very well," the older agent concluded, pulling his colleague by the sleeve.

Suzy understood from the doleful look on the faces of the agents that she had nothing more to fear. They returned her documents to her and departed with nods and forced smiles.

"Where is your baggage?" Miranda asked Suzy in French.

She pointed to the suitcase that had been at the officers' feet.

"That's all? Caetano, put that in the car." He waited until the two officers were at some distance to continue speaking to Suzy in French. In addition to Portuguese, this former Minister of Foreign Affairs spoke French, English, and Spanish. "My name is Santiago Miranda." "Your husband is a colleague," he said to describe their relationship simply. "He asked me to come pick you up. I'm sorry for the delay. I had an important meeting this morning."

Suzy relaxed. "Pleased to meet you, Monsieur. Where is Antonio?"

"His Highness is on a business trip. He'll probably be back tomorrow."

The lawyer knew he mustn't reveal Prince Antonio's secret mission. Suzy would have panicked if she knew his destination was Paris. "He told me he left you a letter at his home," he added. "Let's go. The child must be tired after the journey. What's his name?"

"Rodolfo."

The little boy wasn't paying attention to the talkative man. Captivated by the hustle and bustle of the port, he remained silent, his gaze riveted on the big boats at the pier. Latecomers were running to gangways that were about to be raised, mothers were holding on to their children to keep them from going too close to the pier, and longshoremen were zigzagging through clusters of people saying farewell. Suzy had only ventured out of her cabin twice, to eat, during the journey. Rodolfo hadn't seen so many people since their departure from Marseille.

The limousine headed towards the Baixa neighbourhood. Prince Antonio's apartment overlooked the seashore and the vehicle had to climb up through narrow, winding streets. They made polite conversation in the car. The lawyer tried to reassure Suzy when she asked him where the prince had gone. He claimed not to know all the details of the journey and changed the subject. Now that she was in Lisbon, he said, she should taste the delicious menus of the city's restaurants.

Suzy thanked him, while remaining on her guard. Going from a cramped ship cabin to a chauffeur-driven limousine, she had a feeling of unreality. Was she dreaming or had she actually managed to save her own skin and that of her child?

The car stopped in front of a stylish old building with columns at the entrance and gargoyles on guard at the top. Suzy could tell from the cars parked along the sidewalk that this was an elegant neighbourhood. The lawyer ordered his chauffeur in Portuguese to escort the lady and her child to his apartment and handed him the keys. Carrying the suitcase, Caetano led Suzy and Rodolfo to the fourth floor and unlocked the door. He put the suitcase down at the entrance, handed the keys to Suzy, and said in perfect French, "Welcome to Lisbon." He turned and went quickly back downstairs to drive his boss to his office.

Suzy closed the door and by reflex double-locked it, as she did in her apartment in Paris. She had also locked the door of her cabin on the ship to Lisbon. She looked around the big, orderly living room with its fine furniture. She took a few steps, the child still in her arms. The fireplace in the middle of the room was massive, with a plentiful supply of firewood. However, it wasn't very cold in Lisbon anymore. Spring was coming and the streets were swept by a cool breeze under a warming sun. Sunlight poured in through a big bay window onto the polished wood floor. Outside she could see red tile roofs, an equestrian statue, and in the distance, the blue of the ocean. She contemplated the apartment, whose silence allowed her to calmly take stock of her situation rather than dying little by little in terror. She sank into a chair and allowed the child to explore the room. Tears poured from her eyes and she made no attempt to hold them back.

She finally got to her feet and picked up the little boy again. The child touched her face, surprised by the tears on it. She took hold of his little hands and kissed them.

An envelope was waiting for her on the kitchen counter. It contained a note in English. Antonio welcomed her and hoped that she and their little Rodolfo were well. He apologized for not meeting her at the port, but an urgent matter had to be dealt with. It was a secret mission, and he couldn't say more about it. He added that he had done some shopping and the refrigerator and pantry were well stocked. There were supplies for the child in the bathroom, as well as spring dresses for her in the wardrobe in the master bedroom. He shouldn't be too long, he added. Suzy also found some banknotes in the envelope and contact information for Santiago Miranda in case of emergency.

The Reception Committee at Bourget

Tiago Esteves landed the plane at Bourget without a hitch. His skill and his cool head allowed him to navigate under harassment by a Wehrmacht fighter plane that was following his path over the French capital even though he had received a green light from the Nazis.

He was not hiding his satisfaction at being able to get rid of the "package" Prince Antonio was bringing to the German authorities. When, on departure from Lisbon, he had seen who it was, his blood had run cold. He had immediately recognized Leandro Barros, the head of the Brigada Suprema, and had understood why the prince hadn't wanted to tell him anything ahead of time. He would probably have refused to transport that man, whom he saw as nothing more than a thug. To him, a hero of the Portuguese air force, that character deserved nothing less than the firing squad. He might dress in a uniform and parade around with his buddies, with insignia on his chest and a revolver in his belt, but he wasn't in the military or even in a paramilitary group. He was more like a soldier in an operetta.

Pale as death from his incarceration far from the sun, Barros had waited for the airplane to take off from Lisbon before starting to pester the pilot with questions on his route and his final destination. He knew he was being used as a bargaining chip, but didn't know who Portugal was getting in exchange.

Prince Antonio had explained to him that he was responsible for taking him to join his Nazi colleagues. Germany, he lied, had demanded his release. After that, the journey had continued without further discussion. The prince had spoken to the pilot several times during their Spanish stopover. But Barros hadn't said a word to the African prince. To him, he belonged to an inferior race. He wasn't happy that a Black man was taking him to his Nazi buddies. In fact, he was counting on the German officers on the reception committee at Bourget to arrest the man.

Once on the tarmac, the airplane taxied to a spot indicated by a soldier directing the traffic. An officer of the Wehrmacht came over, accompanied by three soldiers carrying submachine guns. The passengers disembarked, one by one. First the pilot, second the prince, and third the Portuguese fascist, Salazar's former prisoner, who was smiling, happy to be free.

The German officer, a man of average height with a cold stare and a perfunctory smile, gave the Nazi salute and addressed Barros in Portuguese. "Welcome to France, Senhor Barros. Let me introduce myself: Lieutenant Adrian Fischer. We are very pleased by your release. We are aware of the sympathy you have shown with our Führer's cause. I convey warm greetings in his name."

Barros proudly returned the Nazi salute. "I come to express the Portuguese people's unwavering support for Führer Adolf Hitler and to continue the struggle at his side!" He was the shortest man there and his creased suit made him look even more puny. To the officers, he seemed more like an asylum seeker than a fascist leader.

The spectacle disgusted Esteves. He hadn't fought in the Spanish war to be colonized by the Germans. He had joined the Francoist forces because of his anti-Communist convictions. But he had no love for the Nazis. He glared at Barros. "Shut up before I shut you up."

Barros exploded in anger. "You have nothing to say to me! You're Salazar's lackey! You think that in France you can give me orders?"

"Traitor!" retorted the pilot.

Lieutenant Fischer ordered them to stop it. He turned to the prince, "Your Highness Prince Antonio, I presume?"

The prince confirmed his identity, taking out his papers. "Yes, I am. Happy to be back in Paris, although it's only for a few hours." He held out the letter from Santiago Miranda conferring on him the status of Salazar's special envoy.

The lieutenant gave it a quick glance. He had received specific orders from Major Baumeister and had to act quickly. "You're going to the Hôtel Majestic," he said to the prince and the pilot. "My superiors have some questions for you. Guards, bring the car around. We're going to 19 Avenue Kléber!" He said to Barros, "A reception committee will introduce you to the general staff. We'll find you a uniform and insignia worthy of your rank."

Barros thanked him effusively. His obsequiousness caused Esteves to grimace in disgust. He was in a hurry to get away from him. The soldiers clicked their heels and one of them signalled to a car a short distance away on the tarmac. The vehicle, a front-wheel-drive Citroën, sped over. Prince Antonio realized that they were probably going to try to make him confess to trafficking in diamonds. He fingered the laissez-passer in his inside pocket. It was his only hope of returning to Lisbon with Father Eusébio da Silva, the Nazis' prisoner.

The three men got into the Citroën, Barros in front beside the soldier who was driving, the prince and the pilot in back, followed by the Portuguese-speaking Lieutenant Fischer. The lieutenant was holding a pistol.

Another car, a two-door Simca 5, followed them. The prince could make out two men in it, in civilian clothes. He asked Fischer who they were.

"It's the French Gestapo," the lieutenant answered, keeping the Luger in his hand.

The pilot expressed strong disapproval. "We have come under the protection of His Excellency Antonio de Oliveira Salazar. The weapon in your hand is an affront! We wouldn't receive you like that in Lisbon. You should know that we are deeply offended!"

Lieutenant Fischer faked an easygoing smile. "Please don't take it the wrong way. It's strictly to protect us from possible attacks by Communist fanatics. I realize you come from a friendly country."

The two vehicles headed towards the Gestapo office, where Baumeister was waiting for them.

A Long, Anxious Wait

Jean de Dieu and Hans were worried about Prince Antonio. They knew he was in Paris. The two were sitting in the kitchen of the Croissant Doré waiting for the arrival of their friend Jenny. The café was not really a safe place. After all, Hans had killed two policemen who were working for the Gestapo there. But they hadn't had enough time to arrange to meet elsewhere. Jean de Dieu was counting on the fact that the policemen's bodies had never been found to prevent anyone from connecting the missing men to the café. However, Armando had been summoned to report to the judicial police. The Croissant Doré was in the address book of one of the missing men.

The investigation had moved away from the café when two Communists had confessed under torture to the double murder, although they were never able to say where the bodies were. In spite of that, Armando and his friends needed to remain vigilant. He had noticed faces he had never seen before in the café.

Jenny got there ten minutes late. She was wearing a black pinstripe suit. Her wide-collared white shirt was unbuttoned at the neck. She was wearing a hat with feathers. Her skirt went to mid-calf, and wooden-heeled shoes added several centimetres to her height. She greeted Armando and sat down at a table far from curious ears. She put her shoulder bag down and took a packet of cigarettes from the inside pocket of her jacket. That was the signal that she had not been followed and that everything was okay. Jean de Dieu came out of the kitchen in the back and sat down with Jenny. He lit her cigarette. "You're late."

"The Germans seem to be on edge this morning. I had to show my papers several times coming here," she explained in a low voice.

He too had noticed the nervousness of the German soldiers that morning. There was a rumour going around that the German secret service was looking for a clandestine operator in Paris who was communicating in Morse code with London using a two-way radio. "It seems they're looking for a 'pianist,'" he said.

Jenny nodded. She didn't need further explanation. "I can't stay long," she announced, unfolding a Pétainist newspaper. "The package has arrived. It's at the Majestic."

"Shit! He's in the lion's den."

Jenny answered only with a shrug and a sigh.

"You're sure he's there?"

"As sure as day follows night." Jenny gave him a sidelong glance. "I was told by a client. He was trying to impress me."

"They want to question him about his stones," said Jean de Dieu. He bit his lip, concerned.

"Anyway, it doesn't look good. They'll torture him and find out your address."

"He doesn't know where I live. That was deliberate."

"But Prince Antonio knows your real name."

"He won't talk."

"Everybody talks in the end. I think it's time to leave Paris," Jenny whispered.

The suggestion made her lover smile. "I won't leave without him. After all, he came back to get us. His stones are worth a lot of money, but he's risking his life for Hans and me."

Jenny had nothing to say to that.

"If he's in the Majestic for hours, that will mean he's being grilled in the basement. In that case, don't go home. With your real name, they'll end up finding your apartment. Come to my place." She didn't wait for him to answer. "I brought you something to read," she announced, standing up, and pushed her newspaper across the table. The other customers, students with their noses in their books, paid no attention when she winked at him before disappearing into the morning crowds on the way to their factories.

Jean de Dieu put the newspaper under his arm and returned to the kitchen of the café. Hans was waiting there for him, his gaze searching.

Armando joined them, briefly abandoning his customers. Jean de Dieu sat down, looking worried.

"So?" asked Hans.

"I'm afraid the boss has fallen into a trap."

"But he told us he was coming as a special envoy of the Portuguese," said Armando, wiping his hands on his apron.

"Let's go save him," Hans proposed, showing the pistol inside his coat.

"Are you crazy? He's at the Majestic. We wouldn't even get through the door before being gunned down," said Jean de Dieu.

"I have friends who dream of taking on those sadists," said Hans. "With their help and a clever trick, we could do it," said Hans.

Jean de Dieu shook his head. He admired his friend's determination and courage. However, any attempt to get into the Majestic would be suicide. "We have to be more devious than the enemy," he said, opening the newspaper. He found a nice surprise in it. Jenny had written Major Baumeister's private number at the Majestic.

He and Hans looked at each other, impressed. That woman knew how to get what she wanted. She could have dug up the phone number of Goebbels himself.

"You talked about a trick, Hans? How about calling him?" asked Jean de Dieu.

Hans had a good laugh. Armando found the idea inspired. They started discussing the scenario.

Prince Antonio Faces Major Baumeister

The major was standing in the middle of his big office with his arms crossed, a triumphant expression on his face. He had been looking forward to this moment for a long time.

Lieutenant Betz had just handed him the Gestapo's file on Prince Antonio. It contained a ten-page report. There were photographs of meetings with Russian and Swiss businessmen in fancy Parisian restaurants. Allegations of bribery of police officers and accusations of spying for the NKVD. Some informants suggested that he was working for Portugal. However, all this was based on rumour more than anything else. There was no hard evidence to support the various assertions. As for Prince Antonio himself, he claimed he was a student of ethnology.

Baumeister ordered Lieutenant Fischer to stay and translate. Tiago Esteves and Prince Antonio didn't say a word. There were two soldiers standing near them holding automatic submachine guns. The major ordered his men to handcuff the prince.

The pilot, flushed with rage, insisted that the prince be released. "I'll complain to the highest authorities in my country," he exclaimed. "I repeat, this man is a special envoy of the Portuguese government and he enjoys the complete confidence of my president. I demand that you free him immediately!"

After listening to the translation, Baumeister remained impassive. He had the prince in his clutches. That meant he was going to become rich. The prince's diamonds were going to be his. He would sell those gemstones in Latin America. He would disappear without a trace. He was already imagining himself with a Brazilian woman on each arm. He would feel just fine abandoning the army and his wife and daughter. What he wanted was to live a bachelor's life, with tons of money.

Baumeister put the prince's file down on his desk beside the usual three stacks and turned to the aviator. "Captain Tiago Esteves, hero of the war in Spain. They call you the Firebird. I've heard about you and your exploits. It's too bad you agreed to associate yourself with a Black, and even worse, a diamond smuggler. Just be happy I'm not putting you in handcuffs too."

The pilot fumed but didn't answer.

Baumeister nodded to Lieutenant Betz, who told the pilot to follow him. The Firebird tried to protest, but the soldiers with machine guns took a step towards him.

"Go see to your airplane. There must be something you need to do to prepare for takeoff," the major said in German. Fischer translated the order and the pilot understood that it was pointless to resist. He left the office under guard. This was going to end badly, he thought to himself.

Having gotten rid of Esteves, the major concentrated on his prey. "I knew you'd come back," he told the prince, opening his file. "Your name is Antonio Jose Henrique Dos Santos Mbwafu. They call you Prince Antonio and you're of Angolan origin. You say you're a student at the Institut d'Ethnologie de Paris. According to your teachers, you are studious and brilliant. They have nothing but praise for you." The major stopped speaking for a moment to let Lieutenant Fischer translate. "You are also known in the Paris underworld as a notorious diamond smuggler." He showed the prince photos of himself with older men at the Ritz. "Those are your clients. Rich merchants who pay premium prices for the precious stones your father ships you from Angola to the port of Lisbon."

The prince's only comment was to shake his head.

"You're skilful with a blade and you have a reputation of not leaving any embarrassing witnesses alive." the major continued. "If you can't bribe them, you murder them. Do you take issue with any of that, Prince Antonio?"

His Highness waited for the translation. With a sardonic smile, he answered in Portuguese, "First of all, these handcuffs are ridiculous. I don't consider myself a fugitive. I am the emissary of President Salazar, who desires the release of his friend Father Eusébio da Silva. In Paris, I study ethnology. My meetings in those photos are part of my search for patrons to support an ethnological expedition in Africa."

"I'm afraid your reputation as a criminal has preceded you," replied the major.

"I'm not a criminal. I am Prince Antonio, heir to the throne of the Kingdom of Kongo. The accusations against me are unfounded. It's true that I have money. But that's to be expected. I'm the heir to a kingdom rich in diamonds and valuable minerals such as gold."

"Your kingdom has diminished substantially since Portuguese colonization. Soon you will no longer exist."

The prince found that comment highly offensive. Clenching his teeth in scorn, he replied, "The Kingdom of Kongo will be reborn from its ashes once it is liberated from colonization, and it will be one of the richest in the world."

Baumeister looked him in the eye. "Africa will never be free. You are uncivilizable."

A mocking smile played on the prince's lips when he heard Lieutenant Fischer's translation. "We'll see about that," he said.

Baumeister immediately changed the subject. He felt he was losing his grip, far from his basement. The cries of torture victims, the clanking of chains, and the spatters of blood on the walls would have deflated the prince's assurance. "You know what we're looking for. All illegal commercial activity must be punished and the proceeds must be turned over to German justice."

"You've got the wrong man. I repeat, I am a student."

The major didn't listen. "Who are your accomplices? I know you have help in Paris." He placed the composite sketches of Jean de Dieu and Hans in front of the prince.

"They could be anyone," said the prince. "They may be members of my staff. As the representative of the royal family of Kongo, I have been authorized by my father, the venerable Pedro VII, to have a driver and a translator."

Baumeister turned to Betz, who handed him two more files, not as thick. "The translator you are referring to is João de Deus Kassoma, alias Jean de Dieu. I met him once and I mistook him for you. The reason is simple, he's the one who attends classes under your name at the Institut d'Ethnologie and that's why the professors speak of a francophone. According to his papers, he's from Angola, like you. But his French doesn't have the slightest Portuguese accent. Very suspicious."

He looked through the other file. "The second individual is of mixed blood. He's one of those bastards from the Rhineland. He goes by the name Jules Montlouis and hangs around with Caribbean musicians who play that degenerate music they call jazz. He's said to be trigger-happy. Two French police officers who were investigating him disappeared under suspicious circumstances." Baumeister paused for the translation before continuing. "We know his true identity. He's Jakob Moussa Cissé. He entered France illegally in search of his father, a deserter from the French army, a Senegalese soldier who got an Aryan woman pregnant."

The major removed his monocle, blew on it, cleaned it with a white handkerchief, and held it up to the light. "So, now that you know how much information we have on you, I advise you to confess to smuggling precious stones from Angola. The German state will seize your ill-gotten gains as it does with the illegal property of Jews in France. You'll be put on trial. If you cooperate, I may perhaps be able to arrange for you to avoid the firing squad."

The major's accusations didn't rattle the prince. He listened to the translation and shrugged, unimpressed. "I intend to return to Lisbon before nightfall with Captain Esteves." He held his handcuffed hands up in front of the major. "As far as your accusations are concerned, I think it's all a misunderstanding. You've got the wrong man. Africans all look alike to you White people. I've never smuggled diamonds in my life."

Angered, the Nazi officer grabbed Prince Antonio by the collar, crumpling his silk necktie and his expensive coat. "You'll answer me or I'll have you taken to the basement. There, I have other methods of persuasion. A little dandy like you won't be able to hold out for one minute in my hands. I'd be very happy to show you what we call the bathtub. You swallow water until you lose consciousness. So what's your choice?" Fischer hurried to translate.

The prince didn't answer. He was observing the major with pure hatred. He waited for the man to let go. Which Baumeister did, with a look of disdain. Then he wiped his hands on the prince's coat.

Unperturbed, Prince Antonio leaned back in his chair and waited. The major slapped him in the face to wipe away his arrogant expression. The prince remained undaunted.

Baumeister was about to hit him again, this time with the back of his hand, knowing that his death's head ring, a gift from Himmler, would injure the man, but he was interrupted by the ringing of the telephone. He cursed in annoyance and picked up. Magda was at the other end. "I hope this call is of the greatest importance" he exclaimed. "You know how I hate being interrupted when I'm working!"

Magda had to hold the phone away from her head to prevent an earache. "It's a call from the office of President Salazar."

The major's throat constricted. All this for a Black? How could the Portuguese espionage service have obtained his private number? "Put them through."

Magda hurried to comply.

"Major Baumeister?"

"Yes. To whom do I have the honour of speaking?"

"João de Deus Kassoma. Do you remember me? I was in the bath and you made me get out in my birthday suit. I hope I didn't offend your tender sensibilities."

The major was completely taken by surprise.

Hans had spoken to Magda, posing as a German officer and saying that Salazar's personal advisor wanted to talk to her boss. When she heard Armando's accent and his angry tone, she had rushed to transfer the call.

The major realized that his secretary had been hoodwinked. He didn't want to lose control of the interrogation by revealing this to his prisoner or to Lieutenant Fischer, so he played along. "What do you want?"

"Let's get down to business, Baumeister. I'm calling to propose a deal. You have something I want and I have something you want."

"What are we talking about?"

Baumeister's tone and his terse responses made both the prince and Fischer curious. They were listening attentively.

"I have the diamonds," said Jean de Dieu. "That's what you're looking for, isn't it?"

"Yes, exactly."

"I have them in front of me right now. In return, I want a laissez-passer for my friend and one for me. In the names of João de Deus Kassoma and Jules Montlouis. We want to take a little trip to Switzerland. The fresh mountain air will do us good."

The major met the gaze of Lieutenant Fischer, who was trying to understand what kind of scheme was being cooked up. Baumeister was afraid the lieutenant would report everything to his superior. He had already disobeyed General von Bose's orders by handcuffing the prince and roughing him up. He was only supposed to flatter him and bribe him into working for German espionage. "Okay," he said, "I'm listening."

"Take my boss back to his apartment in La Muette. I'll be there with the bag containing the diamonds. You'll give me the laissez-passers there."

Baumeister couldn't alert his superiors. If he did, he would have to turn the diamonds over to the German treasury. He wanted the loot for himself. "Okay, in one hour," he said loudly. "I'll inform General von Bose."

Jean de Dieu knew he would do nothing of the sort. "Let me speak to the prince," he demanded.

"No."

"Let me speak to him. I have to make sure he's alive. Or else no diamonds."

Determined to get his hands on the precious stones, Baumeister gave in. He spoke very loud so that Fischer would hear. "Here's Prince Antonio. He'll tell you himself that everything is okay."

The receiver was handed to the prince, who took it in his two handcuffed hands. Baumeister was expecting Lieutenant Fischer to translate the prince's Portuguese. What a surprise he got when he realized the prince was speaking to Jean de Dieu in an African language! How dare the man speak that barbarian language in his office? Furious, he ordered the lieutenant to take the receiver from the prince. The lieutenant hesitated, because you don't interrupt a call from Salazar's office, even if it's in an African language. He certainly did not want to be at the centre of a diplomatic incident.

"These primitives are nothing but monkeys!" shouted Baumeister. Fischer immediately translated his words into Portuguese, hoping to redeem himself.

Baumeister stood up and snatched the telephone from the prince, who simply smiled and held out his hands for them to remove the cuffs. "Take these off, and keep your hands away from my face," he said.

Baumeister scratched his neck, annoyed. This Black was clearly not afraid of him. But he wanted the diamonds. He motioned to a guard to uncuff the prince.

"So I suppose we don't have to take the prince down to the basement now?" asked Lieutenant Fischer.

The question interrupted Baumeister's calculations. "Lieutenant, I believe it's time for you to return to your post at Bourget," he said. He stood up and nodded towards the door.

"The interrogation is over?"

"Yes. I won't need you anymore."

Fischer gave a formal salute, clicking his heels, and left the office, holding his leather gloves in his right hand. He was relieved that he wouldn't be needed anymore. He would just as soon not have to translate the words of someone being tortured.

The major realized that with Fischer gone, they would have to continue in English. He was able to speak it, but he didn't want to express himself in the language of the enemy. He got Magda to come and translate. She announced to the prince that when they went back to his apartment, the German government would confiscate his diamonds.

The prince smiled enigmatically. "You don't seem to believe I'm just a student of ethnology," he said in English. He adjusted his cufflinks and continued, "A prince never lies, especially not to a beautiful woman."

Magda blushed in embarrassment. This man had an undeniable flair for seduction.

To break the prince's spell, Baumeister issued orders in a peremptory tone. "Call for my car, Magda, and tell Hermann to be ready. I'll go downstairs with the savage."

Magda complied without asking any questions. Baumeister ordered two guards to follow them downstairs and to sit on either side of the prince in the car. He got in next to his driver. Meanwhile, Parisians were going about their business, oblivious to Baumeister's machinations.

They arrived in La Muette without fanfare. Baumeister got out of the car. The guards stayed inside with the prince. The major didn't want to panic the residents of the building. Those diamonds had to be handed over to him without violence. Once they were in his possession, it would be another story. He took the elevator up with Hermann. Neither one said a word. There were two laissez-passers in the pocket of the major's uniform. If he could have gone up to the apartment alone with the prince, he would have done so. But he considered the prince a dangerous man. Hermann was carrying an automatic pistol hidden under his coat. The major had a Luger on his belt. Neither of them was an expert marksman, although they both knew how to use a gun.

Baumeister didn't have time to knock before Hans opened the door, a murderous scowl on his face. He was wearing a black suit, a polka-dot tie, and a Panama hat. "Come in, we've been expecting you," he said in German. His unbuttoned coat revealed his ivory-grip pistol.

When the major saw the pistol, he motioned to Hermann not to react. "Where is Jean de Dieu?" he asked. "He's the one I talked to."

"I'm here," announced Jean de Dieu, elegantly dressed in a khaki suit, white tie, and wide suspenders with silver tips. He looked like a croupier in a casino. His fedora, which he wore at an angle, and the cigarette in the corner of his mouth completed the image of a dandy. Standing in the doorway to the bedrooms of the apartment, he slid a black canvas bag to the middle of the luxurious living room. The metallic sound from inside it made Baumeister and his driver, still in the vestibule, freeze.

The major moved to open the black bag and Hans said, "Don't touch. Where is His Excellency Prince Antonio?"

"Downstairs. You don't think I was going to let him come upstairs with us. That would have made three against two. Don't you know how to count?"

Hans slowly approached the major as if he was going to teach him to be more polite. Hermann stepped between the two men. Hans noticed that he was carrying a weapon too. "Tell your driver not to touch his little toy. Jean de Dieu shoots faster than his shadow."

Jean de Dieu was indeed waiting for the slightest move by Hermann to shoot him down.

The major tried to calm things. "Come now, let's get to the transaction. Once I see the diamonds, Hermann will go downstairs and tell my men to release the prince."

"I see you've thought of everything," commented Jean de Dieu. He stubbed out his cigarette in an ashtray on the windowsill and nodded to the major to come closer to the loot.

Baumeister undid the canvas straps of the bag and opened the leather case inside. He saw a dozen sparkling diamonds and two silver necklaces with green and blue precious stones. He held the stones up to the light and smiled with satisfaction. He knew diamonds, having spent years in Poland looting the valuables of wealthy Jewish families for his generals. There was enough there for him to disappear and live out the rest of his life free from want in a poor country, say in Caracas or Santiago de Chile. As everyone watched, he carefully closed the bag and picked it up.

"Not so fast. The laissez-passers," ordered Jean de Dieu. He had taken out his weapon and was holding it against his leg. Hermann was about to draw his, but Hans already had his ivory-grip 9 mm aimed at his temple. "Don't move," said Hans.

Hermann remained motionless.

"Here are the laissez-passers," said the major, slowly taking the documents out of his inside pocket. "You won't have any problems leaving French territory with these. We'll even form a guard of honour for you." He surprised himself with his quip. He felt satisfied and rich. He deserved this loot. After his years of service tracking down Jews, planning executions, and torturing enemies of the Third Reich, he had been hoping for his reward. He felt he was finally getting his fair share out of this war. He imagined himself in the company of loose women, with champagne flowing freely.

Hermann noticed the pleased expression of his superior. He wasn't used to seeing him with a smile on his lips. He was intrigued by this unusual behaviour.

Jean de Dieu read the documents and said to Hans, "We're important people from the Belgian Congo returning from a conference in Berlin chaired by Himmler!"

Baumeister said, "You're guaranteed to get across the borders. My signature is as good as gold and you have all the necessary stamps." He picked up the canvas bag and turned towards Hermann, who held out his hand to take it. "No, I'm hanging onto it. Go downstairs and order the men to let Prince Antonio come up. Then, wait a few minutes. If I don't come and join you, tell them to come and get me."

"Come now, you ought to trust us. We keep our word," said Hans, lowering his weapon.

Hermann tiptoed around him, afraid to make a false move. He didn't feel up to the task. These two Blacks intimidated him, even though he too had a weapon. He hurried down the stairs to release Prince Antonio.

In the meantime, Baumeister and Jean de Dieu stood watching each other. Hans turned around and followed Hermann without the German realizing it.

The major held the bag against his chest, thinking to himself that these two Blacks were amateurs. Where did they get the idea they could carry this off? Once he was downstairs, he would send his two soldiers up to the prince's apartment. They would pepper the place with bullets, and even the laissez-passers in Jean de Dieu's pocket would be unrecognizable. He would take care of Hermann himself in the car, to eliminate the only witness to the transaction with the Blacks. Then he would call for reinforcements in order to make things official. As for the diamonds, they wouldn't be found. These novices made him laugh. He had no pity for anyone. Captain Tiago Esteves would return to Lisbon with Father da Silva, without the prince. Faced with this fait accompli, General von Bose would have to come up with a diplomatic lie. Baumeister would already be on his way to Buenos Aires under a false identity.

In front of the building, Hermann carried out his instructions in broken English. Prince Antonio still managed to understand him. The prince slowly climbed out of the vehicle, stretched, and adjusted his Panama hat. This irritated Hermann. "Hurry up!" he ordered.

The two soldiers kept their eyes on the prince. That didn't seem to bother him. He exchanged a friendly greeting with a neighbour who was leaving the building, a woman he often encountered in the morning, and then he walked through the front door. Once out of sight, he quickened his pace. He didn't go to the stairwell or the elevator. He slipped out the rear door of the building as Jean de Dieu had instructed him in Swahili when they spoke on the phone in the major's office. Behind the building, he got into a waiting vehicle with Hans behind the wheel.

"Glad to see you again, boss," said Hans. They were speaking English to each other.

"Me too, Hans," replied the prince, and patted him on the shoulder by way of greeting. "Where's Jean de Dieu?"

"He shouldn't be long," said Hans, looking in his rear-view mirror.

Upstairs, Baumeister nodded to Jean de Dieu and left quickly to go to his waiting car. He decided to take the stairs to get down faster. The bag against his right hip, he descended the steps two at a time.

Jean de Dieu went out onto the balcony of the apartment and turned on the prince's fan in front of a pile of papers. He left hurriedly. As he was going downstairs, the fan sent the papers flying over the railing into the air and scattered them in front of the building and on the sidewalk.

Baumeister, sitting in the car, was about to send the two men to empty their machine guns in the prince's apartment, when he saw the papers raining down onto the windshield. They were enlarged photographs, and through the glass he recognized his own face in them. He reached out to grab one and saw that it showed his erotic encounter with Angèle, who had since vanished.

In a panic, he rushed to pick the photos up before they caught the attention of passersby. There were already a good thirty of them under his feet. He looked up and saw that they were coming from the prince's apartment. "Go up there and kill those animals!" he ordered his men.

While his men rushed up the stairs, people across the street had already gotten hold of the photos and had seen the naked major in his frolics. Recognizing him there in uniform, they hurried away with the photos in their hands.

Jean de Dieu, hiding in a dark corner on the ground floor, saw the two soldiers go by and head up the steps, their faces contorted with rage. How could anyone humiliate their leader like that? They were going to make those uppity Blacks pay.

Jean de Dieu emerged from his hiding place and went over to the major's vehicle, his semi-automatic Ruby drawn. "Nobody move. Give me the bag. Hurry up."

Hermann immediately put his hands up. He wasn't going to get himself killed for Major Baumeister.

His superior turned towards him. "Do something! That's an order!"

Hermann read the homicidal intent in Jean de Dieu's eyes. "He's going to shoot, Major! You'd better do what he says."

His reaction enraged Baumeister, who demanded absolute obedience from his subordinates. "Are you out of your mind?" he shouted. "Disobeying a direct order from your superior. You deserve the firing squad!"

But Hermann kept his hands up. He wanted to return to Germany someday, in one piece.

Jean de Dieu pointed his gun at the major, certain that the driver would not play the hero. He picked up the canvas bag at the major's feet and backed away, holding him at gunpoint. Smiling enigmatically, he disappeared into the building.

"You goddamn coward!" shouted Baumeister at Hermann. "Hurry up, catch him! That Black is getting away!"

Hermann realized then that his superior had intended to keep the diamonds for himself. This put an end to any thought of going after Jean de Dieu. On the contrary, he promised himself he would denounce the major at the first opportunity. He had been willing to drive him to visit his lady friends in the evening without informing General von Bose, but helping him steal diamonds was out of the question.

The major realized that his driver had seen through his scheme. He had to act quickly to silence the only witness to his transaction with the Blacks. He drew his Luger and put a bullet in Hermann's head. Some Parisians ran for cover when they heard the gunshot. Others saw him gun Hermann down and kept their distance.

Baumeister tried to catch up with Jean de Dieu, but he ran into the two soldiers coming down the stairs. "There's no one up there, Sir!"

"I know that, you morons! They're getting away!"

They heard Hans's car speed off. They tried to find the rear exit but took a wrong turn. When they finally found the exit, the car was out of sight.

"Come on, we'll go after them," ordered the major, out of breath. There was no time to lose if they were to catch the fugitives.

They rushed to the major's Citroën. There was a crowd around it. People were laughing and talking about the salacious photos. The major fired into the air to drive them away. There was a stampede.

When the crowd had dispersed, there remained two men in the uniform of the Wehrmacht. They were majors, like Baumeister, and they were observing him intently. They had been heading to the site of a train sabotage in the suburbs when they were notified of a suspicious gathering in the 16th arrondissement. They had arrived under heavy escort and observed the crowd of laughing people and the compromising photos.

"Major Baumeister," asked one of them, photos under his feet. "Can you explain to me what's going on here?"

Baumeister recognized him. They had fought in the Poland campaign together. He didn't recognize the other officer. "Major Hoffman, I can explain everything. A Black killed my driver," he said, pointing to Hermann's body nearby.

"That's not what the witnesses are saying," replied Major Hoffman.

"You're not going to believe these people from an inferior race. The word of a major in the Wehrmacht is much more important, as you surely know," replied Baumeister indignantly.

"The passersby are not the only witnesses. We are majors in the Wehrmacht like you. We've been watching you for a while. And you're right, our word is much more important."

Baumeister blanched. He adopted a tone of confidences among colleagues. "I'm about to arrest three dangerous diamond smugglers. If you let me leave with my men, we'll catch them and I'll answer all your questions. You'll see this is all just a misunderstanding."

"What men are you talking about?" asked the second colleague.

Baumeister turned from one side to the other, but his two guards were no longer there. They had blended in with the troops heading to the site of the sabotage. Baumeister found himself alone trying to justify this raid to recover diamonds that no one had ordered him to search for. Then there were those photos of him carrying on stark naked.

"You'll have to turn in your weapon and follow us. I'm sure General von Bose at the Hôtel Majestic will be surprised to see what you've been playing at while we've been dealing with terrorist attacks."

Baumeister imagined the steely blue eyes of the general. Those cold, piercing eyes could kill. It would be the Eastern Front for him—if he didn't end up facing a firing squad. "You're making a mistake—" he began.

But he didn't have time to finish. Two guards came over and disarmed him. They put him in a jeep, his wrists handcuffed behind his back. Headed for the basement of the Hôtel Majestic, his favourite place. But this time, he was the one who was going to be interrogated.

Return to Bourget

Hans drove fast, passing a lot of soldiers along the way. The stolen Citroën had a Portuguese flag on the front fender on the driver's side. Hans had said to himself that it would make the soldiers think twice before stopping them for a check. That worked until they were just a few minutes from their destination. Since they were getting close to an airport, they had to go through a checkpoint.

The prince showed his letter signed by Salazar personally, and the officers on duty were aware that Father da Silva was already waiting on the runway. The two other passengers showed their laissez-passers as attendees returning from a conference in Berlin.

They arrived on the tarmac, where Tiago Esteves, Father Eusébio da Silva, and Lieutenant Fischer were waiting. This time, there was just one guard present. The priest was relieved to see the prince. He wanted to leave as quickly as possible, before the Nazis changed their minds. Everything took place in Portuguese.

"You had me scared! We were supposed to leave an hour ago," said the priest.

Captain Esteves climbed out of the cockpit, where he was checking the instruments. Smiling broadly, he embraced the prince. "Dammit, Prince Antonio, you're one tough cookie."

"Sorry for the delay," said the prince. "I had to explain myself to the authorities. But everything's taken care of now."

"Where's Major Baumeister?" asked Lieutenant Fischer, looking into the empty car.

"Something came up at the last minute. He said he has complete confidence in you to instruct the control tower to let us take off. I'm bringing two diplomats with me who are returning from a conference in Berlin."

Fischer consulted the travel manifest. "That was not planned."

"Come now," said the priest, "you're not going to hold us here because of that!"

The lieutenant read the laissez-passers for Jean de Dieu and Hans. The news of Baumeister's arrest hadn't reached him. He stamped the documents and signalled the guard to give the control tower the green light.

The pilot rubbed his hands together. "We'll be able to go back to Portuguese cuisine. You must have missed it, my dear Father."

They boarded the Caudron C.440. The lieutenant noticed that Jean de Dieu and Hans had no baggage. He concluded that they must be secret agents, but he didn't want to get involved. Baumeister was in charge of espionage and counter-espionage, not him. He mustn't make waves if he wanted to avoid going to fight the Russians. "Have a good trip," he said in Portuguese. He turned and walked away, off the runway.

Tiago Esteves started the engines, and a few minutes later the airplane took off.

When the Firebird confirmed that they were over Spain, a huge wave of relief swept through the passengers. The priest insisted that they say a prayer. The prince lit a cigar although it was not permitted to smoke during flight. He thought about Suzy and the little prince he was going to be reunited with in Lisbon. In his pants pocket were the coveted diamonds and the necklaces. Jean de Dieu thought about his last night with Jenny. It couldn't be the end for them. She would have to join him. If necessary, he would go get her. Hans wondered if he would find interesting jazz bars in Lisbon. His boss had promised him a new saxophone. His old one was beginning to show traces of tarnish from being dragged around to so many poorly heated rooms. As for Jean de Dieu, Prince Antonio had offered him a new bookshelf of volumes on ethnology, philosophy, and literature. After all, those two men had saved the two persons who were dearest to him in the world.